Track Down Borneo

A Brad Jacobs Thriller

__Book 5__

SCOTT CONRAD

PUBLISHED BY:
Scott Conrad
2nd Edition © June 2018
Copyright © 2018-2019
All rights reserved.

No part of this publication may be copied, reproduced in any format, by any means, electronic or otherwise, without prior consent from the copyright owner and publisher of this book.

This is a work of fiction. All characters, names, places and events are the product of the author's imagination or are used fictitiously.

A Brad Jacobs Thriller Series by Scott Conrad:

TRACK DOWN AFRICA – BOOK 1
TRACK DOWN ALASKA – BOOK 2
TRACK DOWN AMAZON – BOOK 3
TRACK DOWN IRAQ – BOOK 4
TRACK DOWN BORNEO – BOOK 5
TRACK DOWN EL SALVADOR – BOOK 6
TRACK DOWN WYOMING – BOOK 7

Visit the author at: ScottConradBooks.com

Come on, you sons of bitches! Do you want to live forever?

GySgt. Daniel J. "Dan" Daly, USMC

near Lucy-`le-Bocage as he led the 5th Marines' attack into Belleau Wood, 6 June 1918

Table of Contents

Prologue 1

One.. 4

Two.. 18

Three...39

Four...51

Five..67

Six..87

Seven.. 105

Eight... 124

Nine 141

Ten...154

Eleven... 168

Twelve 185

Thirteen..204

Fourteen...228

Fifteen 239

Sixteen..269

Seventeen 303

Eighteen 324

Nineteen 350

Twenty 381

Twenty-One 393

PROLOGUE

PRESENT DAY

William Darnell Duckworth IV, "Bill" to his very few friends and CEO of Duckworth International Petroleum to everyone else, landed at Brunei International Airport (*Lapangan Terbang Antarabangsa Brunei*) in Bandar Seri Begawan and was immediately bowled over by the opulence of the ultramodern facility. He had known there was big money in Brunei, but he had not known that the benefits of that prosperity were extended to the masses there. It was patently obvious to him that the dossier compiled for him by his staff had been woefully inadequate, and he resolved to do some research of his own as soon as he was settled in his suite at the Empire Hotel & Country Club in Bandar Seri Begawan.

An unsmiling man in a black chauffeur's livery and bearing a neatly printed cardboard sign with

"Duckworth" on it greeted him the instant he exited the jetway and escorted him out to a gleaming black stretch limousine with dark tinted windows. The chauffeur opened the door for him and closed it behind him. Bill set his briefcase on the seat beside him and opened it, beginning to reread the heads of agreement prepared for him by his staff for the joint drilling venture with the government of the Sultanate of Brunei. He paid little attention to the sights outside the limousine as it entered and emerged from a large traffic circle and turned onto a large modern four-lane highway. He looked up from his documents and noticed a massive stadium off to his right just before the limo entered into another traffic circle and turned onto a much narrower two-lane street. When he glanced back down at the documents, he didn't notice the trees and greenery closing in towards the sides of the roadway.

The limo suddenly screeched to a halt, all four tires locking up. He heard shouting and then saw the limo driver opening the front door and diving out. A split-second later all the rear doors were jerked open and several men armed with AK-47s and dressed all in black swarmed inside the limo and wrestled him to the floorboard. Just before he lost consciousness he realized that the handkerchief they were holding over his nose smelled like chloroform.

ONE

Willona Ving stared down at the spreadsheets on the desk in front of her for the umpteenth time and bent forward to rest her head in her hands. The numbers didn't lie, and they were telling a story that she wasn't comfortable with at all. The newly formed Jacobs & Ving Security LLC was not broke, but it did not have the operating capital that it needed to finance the type of large-scale operations that were its bread and butter. The last three jobs had generated little or no revenue, and in fact had made deep inroads on Brad's reserves.

Brad Jacobs had enlisted in the U.S. Marine Corps right out of high school. His father, a career Marine, had been killed at the end of the Gulf War during Operation Desert Storm. His own experience in the Corps had molded him into a Marine recruiting poster of a man, a man who embodied the ideals and the very spirit of the Corps. He was not only a battle hardened professional with extensive experience in Special Operations, he looked the part as well. Six feet two inches tall with a muscular build and a blond, military style buzz cut, he had a lantern jaw and sea-green eyes. He exuded self-confidence and had an unmistakable aura of inner strength. Willona had known him her entire married life, and she knew Brad lived by his own rigid inner code. She admired the man almost as much as she admired her husband, Mason.

Mason Ving, a retired forty-eight-year-old Force Recon gunnery sergeant, was a massive man, six feet tall and two hundred and sixty pounds of muscle, tendon, and bone. He had acquired a small pot belly since his retirement from the Corps, but it hadn't slowed him down any. His skin was so black that it had blue highlights in the light of day, and his bald head shone in any kind of light. His smiling brown eyes could turn deadly and reptilian when he was pissed, and his friends had learned over time that when his eyes went flat, it was best to be anywhere else. It was not as if the man couldn't be friendly; he had a deep, warm voice that wasn't at all what one would expect to hear coming from the mouth of a Force Recon gunnery sergeant, it sounded remarkably like the voice of the actor James Earl Jones. When he did get riled, that same voice could sound as if it was coming from the lungs of the devil himself, but that didn't happen very often. His sheer bulk and his attitude were intimidating enough to cover most circumstances, even in the heat of battle ... but with Willona and the kids he was a gentle bear of a man.

The two men had served together in Force Recon and had become tighter than blood brothers. After separating from the Corps, the two had teamed up to work as bounty hunters, but their growing reputation had resulted in their being sought out by corporate entities who were dealing with modern terrorist groups that had discovered a remarkably profitable revenue generating scheme—kidnapping vital executives and holding them for ransom. Brad, Ving, and their little band of comrades had earned a respect bordering on reverence over time, and their services commanded a premium rate … but not as much as the corporations would have been willing to pay, which was one of several things Willona was going to have to take up with Brad and her husband.

"Oh Brad," she murmured into the emptiness of the private office she maintained in her own home, "how have you managed all these years without me?" His record keeping was execrable, and he apparently had done his own tax returns over the last few years. It was manifestly obvious that he had vastly overstated his income on his returns because he did not understand or claim most of the deductions allowed him under the tax laws. Willona sat up and reached for her cell phone, punching the speed dial button for her accountant.

"Hannah? Willona. Listen; remember me telling you I talked Ving into investing in his best friend's business?" She sat silently for a few seconds. "Yes, we did, and I insisted on being named chief financial officer ... and it's a good thing I did. I've been going over the spreadsheets and you aren't going to believe what I've found. He's been doing his own tax returns, and the man doesn't have any inkling as to what he's entitled to as far as deductions." She listened a bit longer. "Yes Hannah, overpaid by so much that I'm having trouble believing he hasn't been audited." She rested her chin on one hand for support as she listened a little longer. "We're going to need your whole team, Hannah. We will need to file amended returns for as far back as the IRS will allow, and they're going to scream bloody murder at having to give all that cash back. The revenue stream is impressive, and I think that with some solid fiscal policy and some controls in place this investment is going to be good for all of us ... very good."

* * *

She took her new job seriously, and over the next few weeks she threw herself enthusiastically into it the way she had thrown herself into every endeavor she had engaged in since she and Ving had gotten married so many years before. It had taken some doing to get Brad and Ving out from underfoot so that she could do everything she needed to do. But she had finally gotten truly inspired, bought six large bottles of Brad's favorite imported Belgian beer, and ordered pizza ... double bacon on Ving's. She'd enlisted Vicky Chance to aid her in executing her scheme, which had been one of the smartest things she could have done.

Vicky, a sultry redhead with an extensive military, intelligence and law enforcement background of her own, had met Brad in Cabo San Lucas when the team was prepping for a mission to the Amazon to repatriate Ving's brother. The chemistry between the two had been enormous, and Vicky had quickly become an accepted member of the team ... and Brad's significant other.

The evening had been perfect. Ving had polished off his own large personal pepperoni, bacon, and mushroom pizza and he and Brad were swigging beer while watching Vicky with Jordan and Nathaniel, Ving's sons, chasing fireflies in the backyard.

Willona finished throwing away the cardboard cartons the pizzas had come in and then glanced out at her husband and his partner sitting at the picnic table Ving had built for her. "No time like the present," she muttered, reaching in the refrigerator for one of the large bottles of beer. She removed the small wire basket covering the top and popped out the cork. Carefully pouring herself a glass so as not to disturb the yeast settled in the bottom, as Brad had taught her, she then walked out onto the back patio to take a seat opposite Ving and Brad. She took the rest of the bottle with her in case the guys needed a refill.

"We need to talk, boys," she said, taking a swallow from her glass. "Brad, you've developed a hell of a business over the years."

"Thanks Willona," Brad remarked, one eyebrow arched. "But…?"

"Uh-oh," Ving said, his shoulders hunching defensively, "Duck Brad, I know that look. I usually only see it when she's about to tell me how I screwed something up."

Willona gave her husband a withering glance. Ving's mouth snapped shut, but he was grinning.

She turned her attention back to Brad.

"You don't seem to have any trouble at all getting offers of employment."

"We do have something of a reputation for success, Willona, but I still hear a 'but' in your voice."

"I've done a great deal of research on this subject, and I've conducted several phone interviews, Brad. Did you know that most of your competitors have a business manager and a full-time office staff?"

Brad looked surprised.

"No I didn't realize that, but it seems like that would be kind of expensive. I've gotten along just fine without a bunch of hangers-on, Willona."

"You're missing the point, Brad. Did you know that virtually all your competitors are paid significantly higher rates than you are and none of them have a success rate that even approaches yours?"

Brad actually blushed; then he shrugged.

"They offer me money and I take it. It's never really seemed important. What's important to me is that they need me and they need what my team can do."

"Brad, think of the time you could save, in addition to the money you could make, if you had a support staff. What if all you had to do was plan and execute your missions?"

"I've always managed before, Willona."

"You could get to your clients faster, recover them sooner, and get back home quicker if you had a support staff, Brad."

Brad's brow furrowed in concentration. "Where would they work, Willona? We barely have enough room in my apartment for team meetings and mission briefings."

"That's another thing we need to discuss. You need more space, and your equipment is scattered over four counties …. that I know of. You've got records of purchases of weapons, equipment, and vehicles but no comprehensive listing of assets … and that leads us to all the tax deductions you're entitled to and not taking. Did you realize that you have paid an enormous amount of taxes on income that was not taxable?"

Brad and Ving both looked surprised.

"I need you to do two things, Brad. First, I need you to write down the locations of everywhere you have equipment stashed, and give me the keys. Second, I need you and Ving to take Jordan and Nathaniel on a fishing trip and leave Vicky and me alone to take an inventory. There is a ton of organizational work that needs to be done to get this business on a firm financial footing, and it's my responsibility as chief financial officer to do it."

"She's good at that," Ving offered.

"Yeah, I know she is. I should have asked her advice a long time ago."

"One more thing, Brad... You keep accepting contracts, but from now on, I negotiate the fees."

Ving guffawed so loudly that Vicky and the boys looked back at them from out in the yard.

"This is gonna be funny, Brad. Them boys got no idea what they gonna be facin'. Willona is a real hardass when it comes to squeezin' a dollar."

Willona gave her husband a dirty look, but it didn't cow him in the least. Then she turned to Brad before he could come up with some kind of excuse, but he saw the determination in her face and his mouth snapped shut. It was all he could do to refrain from saying, "Yes ma'am."

* * *

Vicky walked into the bedroom carrying two slender flutes of champagne just as Brad came out of the bathroom, still drying himself with a towel after his shower. She set them down on the bedside table and walked over to him, snatching the towel out of his hands and finishing the job of drying him off.

"Asking Willona to be your CFO was a stroke of genius," she said.

Brad chuckled. "I didn't exactly ask her you know. She sort of presented the idea to me as a *fait accompli.* If I had thought it out, I would have offered Ving a full partnership instead of a quarter of the company. I would never have been able to accomplish the missions I've taken on without him. Ving is my brother, my good right arm." He shook his head. "I still can't figure out how she figures a quarter share of this new company is worth that much money."

"It's worth far more than that, Brad, and Willona knows it. That is one shrewd businesswoman and you're lucky to have her. If you and Ving don't screw it up, she's going to make you very wealthy men."

"I don't do this for the money Vicky," he said solemnly. "I do it because those people need me and because I can't *not* do it."

"I know that, Brad, but just think about it: you can do more, better, and faster if you are better organized and better funded. Honestly, getting Willona Ving to be your CFO is probably the best thing that's ever happened to you."

Brad gave her a long, piercing look and then dropped the damp towel on the floor.

"Make that the second best thing," he said as he leaned forward and took her into his arms.

TWO

While Willona and Vicky conducted the inventory, Brad and Ving loaded up Jordan and Nathaniel and took them camping at Grapevine Lake. Ving favored the Murrell Park Campground inside the city of Flower Mound because it had plenty of unimproved campsites without electricity and because they could pitch a tent right next to the water, and Brad thought it would be a great opportunity to teach the boys how to fish as well as learn some woodcraft skills. The boys were delighted.

Ving was supervising the boys as they cleaned and filleted the fish they had caught on the third day at the site, and Brad was leaning back against a log sipping at a cold dark stout as he watched them. Despite the fact that it had been a long, hot day, he had already started a campfire and was watching it burn merrily down into hot coals to cook over. His stomach was rumbling in anticipation of a fresh fish dinner when his cell phone rang. Willona.

"Yeah," he answered, grinning at Ving's antics, which had both boys roaring with laughter. "Make it quick, Willona, Ving is putting on a helluva show and I don't want to miss any of it."

"Brad, I've got a Mr. Grainger of Duckworth International Petroleum on hold, and I'm about to hook him up with you. I want you to listen to what he says and tell him whether you want the job or not … then, if you say yes, I want you to let me negotiate the fee while you do whatever you need to do. Got it?"

"Sure Willona, put him on."

He heard the click as Willona added Grainger to the call.

Track Down Borneo

"Brad Jacobs, this is Mr. Howard Grainger of Duckworth International Petroleum. Mr. Grainger, this is Brad Jacobs, our president and CEO."

Grainger had a South Texas drawl but spoke articulately and precisely.

"Mr. Jacobs, I'm going to cut to the chase. You come highly recommended to us by a business associate, Jack Paul. I made a few phone calls to people who ought to know, and they tell me you're the best … and that means you are the man I'm looking for."

"Please, call me Brad, Mr. Grainger. Why don't you tell me what the problem is and I'll let you know if I can help?" Brad spoke crisply and firmly, unconsciously sitting up straighter and setting his beer down on the ground beside him as if Grainger could see through the phone.

"Brad, our president, Mr. William Darnell Duckworth IV, was taken from Brunei International Airport in Bandar Seri Begawan day before yesterday by some people who claim to be members of *Jemaah Islamiyah,* you know anything about them?"

"Yes, I do. JI is a jihadist group in Southeast Asia looking to establish a caliphate there by violent activity. They planned and effected a series of terrorist ops, including the Bali bombings in 2002 and 2005 as well as a bunch of bombings in Indonesia and the Philippines. They've also been getting laundered money from al-Qaeda. I hadn't heard of them being active in Brunei, though I do know they have been active in Kalimantan, the Indonesian part of the island of Borneo."

Brad heard the relief in Grainger's voice. "Jack was right about you. He said you were a gold mine of information about terrorists in that part of the world."

"It's my business to know that kind of information, Mr. Grainger. Tell me, have you heard from Mr.

Duckworth's captors yet? Have they demanded any ransom?"

"Yes, they've been in contact with us. They're demanding a hundred million dollars in cash, and initially they only gave us a week to get it together and get it to them, but our legal representatives are experienced at this sort of thing and they have negotiated for an extra week."

"You sound like you have a lot of faith in your negotiators."

"I do. Before they worked for us they worked for the C.I.A. They're an experienced team; they've done this kind of work before."

"I don't understand, Mr. Grainger. If you have a team already why do you need mine?"

"They don't do hands-on, Brad. They negotiate; they handle payments and funds transfers, that sort of thing. They don't do what they refer to as 'wet work' … and they are telling me this one is different. They're saying the abductors are going to kill Bill Duckworth whether we pay them or not."

* * *

They had broken camp in record time, much to the disappointment of Jordan and Nathaniel. Ving had calmed the boys, promising to bring them back to Grapevine Lake after he returned. The boys, used to Daddy's frequent "deployments", which was the way Ving chose to describe the missions he went on with Brad, soon settled into the back seat with their headsets and video games.

"Duckworth International has a team of lawyers and intelligence people, negotiators with Company experience, and they've determined that Duckworth has been taken to an unknown location in Kalimantan, the Indonesian southern part of the island of Borneo. Evidently the JI assholes failed to deactivate Duckworth's satellite phone until he'd been held captive for several hours."

"Seems awfully bush league for a hard-core terrorist organization to me, Brad. JI is bad news; they've planned and executed some pretty serious ops. This doesn't sound like them at all." Ving sounded worried.

"I don't know, Ving, they've had their ups and downs in Indonesia lately. I'd be willing to bet they have a lot of new recruits, guys who haven't been fully trained yet."

Ving frowned and shrugged. It wasn't like Brad to make assumptions on missions, but they hadn't reached his computer and information sources yet, so he would withhold judgment.

"Grainger says that ongoing negotiations have stalled and the J.I. kidnappers seem more interested in making a political statement than in collecting the ransom money."

"That doesn't sound like them either, buddy. There's something more going on here than we're being told."

"I think you're right, Ving, but Willona says she's gonna buy us some time to look into things before we have to commit, and from what she said to me, this looks like it's going to be a really big payday."

Ving grunted noncommittally. For the first time since he'd known Brad, he had real doubts about a mission … but he had limitless faith in Brad.

* * *

Brad, Ving and the boys made it back to Ving's house in good time.

After fending off Grainger's insistence on an immediate response, Willona agreed to give the man an answer within forty-eight hours after he had insisted that he would seek another contractor if she did not respond within that time frame.

"I'm not sure you should take this one, Brad," she told him. "Something doesn't feel kosher about it, but I'll be the first to admit I don't know much about this sort of thing."

"You bought us two days, Willona. We have resources…"

Willona took a deep breath.

"You want me to go ahead and prep for this one anyway?"

"If it turns out to be legit, we'll have to be ready to go wheels up as soon as you tell the guy we're in, so, yes, we need to go ahead and prep." Vicky spoke up for the first time.

Willona glanced over at Ving, who nodded solemnly.

"I don't like this, Ving," she said, "but you guys are the pros and I trust you to know what you're doing." She bunched her fists and planted them solidly on her hips. "If I'm going to calculate a reasonable fee for this goat roping I need some information ASAP. I've seen bits and pieces of how you prepare for an op over the years, but I've never seen it all the way through. I need to know what everyone is doing, but I'll try to keep the questions to a minimum so I don't get in your way." Brad gave her a questioning look. "I need to calculate exactly how much we need to get upfront so that you don't have to come out of pocket to mount your operation. Businesses regularly charge a retainer. All of your competitors do," she added, a bit defensively.

Brad was getting schooled, and he wasn't quite sure how to take it.

"How do you know so much about my 'competitors' so quickly, Willona?"

She gave him an odd look.

"I *Googled* it and visited their websites," she said with a shrug, as if she was surprised that he would ask the question.

"Websites?" he asked, mystified. Vicky choked back her laughter and Ving smirked. Brad was aware that there were other men like him, men who had cut their teeth on Special Operations and responded to calls for help from members of the international business community, but he'd always considered them more as members of an elite fraternity than as competitors. He was not naïve by any stretch of the imagination; he'd just never given it much thought. The truth was he did what he did because he loved it and he was good at it. That he was making his living at it had always been an afterthought.

"I haven't even looked at your website yet, Brad; I've been busy going over the books, which, by the way, need considerably more attention than you've been giving them."

He didn't have the heart to tell her that the only 'advertising' he'd ever done was by word of mouth through China Post #1 in Exile. China Post 1 is an American Legion post, the only post within the legion functioning in exile. The post was formed in 1919 in Shanghai and used the American Club as its headquarters. In the late 1940s, the civil war between the communists and the nationalists forced the Post to evacuate Shanghai. In 1948, they sent their records to the American Legion National Headquarters in Indianapolis and went into exile. China Post 1 is currently an element of the Department of France and a member of the Foreign Departments and Posts of The American Legion. They have no permanent location, though they maintain administrative offices and a post office box in Henderson Nevada. The Post has designated "watering holes" scattered around the world, a list of which is on their website. Members keep in contact through a newsletter and their website. Brad had never even considered building a website even though he used the internet extensively in his research.

"I know you have to make your plans for personnel, weapons, and travel based on your operations order, Brad, but I'm going to need ballpark figures on how many people, distances to be traveled, stuff like that, in order to come up with an estimate for the retainer."

"I don't know, Willona," Brad said doubtfully, "I've never required any money upfront, and I'm not sure how that's going to go over…"

Vicky spoke up.

"Listen to her, Brad. You live in a different world than those guys do. Those guys spend more money on a manicure and a haircut than you do to rent this apartment for a year. Duckworth Petroleum is headquartered in Midland, Texas, and they made billions of dollars last year. As I seem to recall, Bill

Duckworth is the heart and soul of that company, and they can't do without him."

"Vicky and I can go ahead and finish the inventory of your weapons and other assets while you go ahead and decide what to do about this mission, Brad, but you need to get cracking. Time is money!" Willona crooked a finger at Vicky, who gave Brad an amused smile and a peck on the cheek before following the woman into the house.

Ving took one look at the expression on Brad's face and roared with laughter.

"She's a handful, brother, but she's never led me wrong. Look what she's done for me." He shook his head ruefully. "Who woulda ever guessed back in Fallujah that I would one day have enough cash to buy into an outfit like the one we've cobbled together?" He was referring back to the second battle of Fallujah, a crucible where the final link in their unusual bond had been formed.

Brad grunted. "Who would have ever guessed we'd still be doing shit like this all these years later?" He tilted his beer bottle up to his lips and finished it off, then set it down and reached into his pocket for his keys. "I need to get over to my apartment. Apparently I need to get a buttload of information together for my new chief financial officer in a hell of a hurry. You coming?"

"Not right now, brother, somebody has to keep an eye on the boys." He reached for another beer. "I can do that from right here, and if you need me, I'm just a phone call away." He reached into his own shirt pocket and pulled out his Team Dallas BlackBerry, waving it at Brad.

*   *   *

"You know," Willona said, taking a look around, "in all the years I've known you, Brad, I've never been in here before."

The room Brad had set aside in his apartment for his office had originally been a walk-in closet, but up until the present it had always been adequate for his needs. When Vicky had joined the team, he had been forced to conduct more of his work in the living room, especially when all the members of the team were present. Willona's addition to the team—and the amount of money she had paid for the partnership—had forced him to think about her statement regarding his need for a suitable space for the business. With his relationship with Vicky becoming more important to him, he had realized that it was time to take a more professional approach to his career. He had always been a consummate professional, and it struck him as odd that he had taken such a careless attitude towards the business side of what he did. Perhaps it really was time for a change.

"I know, Willona, and I'm beginning to think you're right about my needing a real office, someplace I can do everything I need to in one spot, somewhere I can have everything I need to plan a mission and conduct briefings."

"Good! We can talk more about that later, Brad, but right now we need to put together a bid for this job."

"A bid? I thought they already offered us the job."

"They did, but we haven't accepted it yet. You've got to start taking a different attitude towards your work, Brad. You've made some serious inroads on your cash reserves over those last three missions … you've spent more than two thirds of what you had in those three missions alone. Do you realize that just one more mission like that could break you?"

"I know, but with what you and Ving paid to buy in—"

"Forget about that money, Brad. That and what you had left are your reserve, for emergency only. Think of it as the cornerstone of Jacobs & Ving

Security LLC. We've paid off your credit cards, so you have those, and there's a hundred thousand or so in your personal checking and savings accounts. I'm not going to hassle you about that, that's your business. Your business accounts are a different matter. I set up business checking and savings accounts and I've applied for and gotten credit cards in the company's name for you, Vicky, Ving, and me. We can get others for the rest of the team if you like."

She stopped, taking a breath and watching Brad's face to see how he was taking everything she was throwing at him. Seeing no reaction, she forged ahead. "What we have to do now is get some working capital in those accounts, and that's what we're going to accomplish with the retainer." She opened a manila folder and took out a crisp, clean, neatly typed sheet of paper and presented it to him.

Brad's eyes bulged when he saw the amount of the retainer.

"Jesus Willona, that's more than I expected to get for the whole job!"

"Take it easy, baby," Vicky said soothingly. "I've seen Willona's figures for the whole job and I think twenty-five percent is more than fair."

"Twenty-five percent!" Brad sputtered. "No way they're going to pay that much. That's crazy!" Ving was looking at the figures, too, and he was just as bug-eyed as Brad.

"They not only can, but they will, Brad," Vicky said calmly.

Willona had established a base amount for the budget and then tripled it. Brad and Ving were shocked, but Vicky had agreed with her.

"Brad, you've been badly undercharging your clients. Look at this," she said, pulling a copy of

Duckworth's last annual profit-and-loss statement, which showed a very healthy profit of several billion dollars. Then she took out a segment of their expense statement that showed Duckworth's personal salary, which was more than ten times the amount of the total fee she had arrived at for the entire mission.

Brad shook his head.

"I don't think they'll go for it, but I trust you, Willona. Go for it." He leaned back in his chair and gestured towards the landline on his desk.

Willona sat on the corner of his desk and punched in the number for Grainger's direct line. She pushed the button to turn on the speaker. Grainger picked up the phone on the first ring.

"Mr. Grainger? Willona Ving of Jacobs & Ving Security."

"I've been waiting for your call, Mrs. Ving. I hope you've called to say you've accepted the job, we've all been very anxious here…"

"I have, Mr. Grainger, provided our terms are acceptable to you."

"Let's hear them then."

Willona stated the amounts for the retainer and the total job, with the caveat that extraordinary expenses would be added to the final bill. Grainger never hesitated.

"Fax me over the terms, Mrs. Ving, and I'll sign and return it. If you'll provide me the routing and transmittal numbers, the retainer will be in your account by the time you receive your copy. In the meantime, here is the number and a point of contact for our Crisis Management Team…"

THREE

Despite the urgency of the situation, Brad realized that his knowledge of Borneo and the Jemaah Islamiyah (JI) was extremely limited and probably outdated. He knew that the group was associated with al-Qaeda, with the Abu Sayyaf Group (ASG), a Philippines-based terrorist outfit, and with the Nusra Front. After a long, hard night of research, he learned that JI was a jihadist group located all over Southeast Asia working toward forcibly creating a caliphate in the region. The caliphate, an Islamic state to be called *Daulah Islamiyah Nusantara,* was to encompass Indonesia and Mindanao (southern Philippines), and then gradually absorb southern Thailand, Singapore, and Brunei.

The group was commanded by Abu Bakar Bashir, a co-founder who'd sworn allegiance to ISIS in July of 2014. JI had first gotten global recognition after it executed bombing attacks in Bali in 2002 and

2005, killing two hundred and two citizens and twenty foreign nationals. JI was also known for its ties to the 1993 World Trade Center bombing and the 1995 "Bojinka" scheme, which had been a failed attempt to blow up a dozen U.S. commercial aircraft over a two-day period.

After considerable effort, Brad located a copy of JI's ideological and tactical manual, *General Guidelines of the Struggle of Al Jemā'ah Al Islāmiyah (PUPJI),* online, which gave him a surprisingly detailed picture of JI's organizational structure. The manual divided the group's areas of operation into regions, or *mantiqis*, each having a different administrative or operational purpose. Each *mantiqi* was split into smaller wards, called *wakalahs.*

Mantiqi I functioned in Singapore and Malaysia and served as JI's revenue source, out of which they financed their operations. *Mantiqi II* covered Indonesia, the primary base from which they carried out most of their overt terrorist activities, like launching attacks on government and law enforcement. *Mantiqi III* was comprised of the Philippine island of Mindanao, the Malaysian state of Sabah on the island of Borneo, and the Indonesian island of Sulawesi, where covert training cells were located. *Mantiqi IV*, encompassing Australia and the West Papua province of Indonesia, focused its efforts on fundraising.

Faced with such an enormous glut of information, Brad reached for his cell phone to ask Vicky if there was any way she could help him analyze it all and put it into some sort of understandable form. It didn't sit well with him to have to ask for help, but he knew that even the best commanders had to rely on their team members for intelligence matters, even if it was only for the sake of having a different point of view, perhaps spotting something that the commander might have overlooked.

The call went straight to Vicky's voice mail, and, in frustration, Brad punched the disconnect button on his BlackBerry and brooded for a moment.

"Ah crap!" he muttered to himself. "She and Willona are at the warehouse taking inventory. I should have known better!" The warehouse held more equipment than even Brad could remember. All of it had been left over from prior missions, stashed and forgotten in the aftermath and letdown on the team's return. Specialized cold weather gear and weapons from the Alaskan mission, jungle gear from Africa and the Amazon, desert gear from Iraq; all of it had been thoroughly cleaned and packed away, he was too much of a professional to leave it dirty, but it had been stacked away in the warehouse and forgotten then. It had been far easier to shop for new equipment than it would have been to go through the stacks and dig out what he needed. Willona had been right. For all his skills as a commander and a leader, he'd not given enough thought to the business end of his occupation.

As much as it pained him, he was going to have to realize that if he wanted to continue his successful operations, he was going to have to recognize and accept his responsibilities as a corporate executive. The members of Team Dallas were, to all intents and purposes, full-time employees, and they looked to him for more than just tactical leadership. The sheer magnitude of the concept threatened to swamp him. So many things he had never even thought about slammed around in his head like rabid squirrels on steroids; benefit packages, 401Ks, workmen's compensation, unemployment insurance, the list was endless.

He glanced down at the manila folder on top of his desk that contained the purchase agreement Willona had given him to sign the night he had sold a quarter interest in his 'business' to her and Ving, and then he smiled. Willona was his chief financial officer. Not only was she tough as hell, she was a regular genius when it came to business.

A lecture from his NCO Academy days came back to him. It had been given by a crusty Marine lieutenant colonel who looked as if his face had been carved out of granite and whose utilities had been tailored to fit his impressive physique. Brad remembered that, at the time, he had been totally awed by the man as an officer and a Marine—a Marine's Marine. The colonel had told the group of NCOs that they were the backbone of the Corps and that a truly good leader knew and trusted the capabilities of his NCOs and utilized their individual skills to the best benefit his unit. Only foolish leaders failed to delegate authority ... and only fools believed they could delegate responsibility.

"Trust your subordinate leaders, men ... but don't forget to keep an eye on them. People do what you *inspect*, not what you *expect*. Micro-managers get their people killed in combat ... and that is inexcusable." The colonel's words had stuck in Brad's mind, and they had been invaluable in Force Recon. It struck him as odd that he had never considered applying them to the work he was doing now. He had taken advice from all of them in the past, but he had never really considered breaking down the elements of a mission and assigning them to the team members ... even though he had always used his subordinates that way in the Corps when writing an op order.

He felt as if a great weight had slipped off his shoulders. Willona had proven herself in the world of business and money. He would watch and learn, but he would let her run the business end. Relieved, he turned his mind back to assimilating all the information he had gathered from the internet. Within minutes he was mentally kicking himself. Vicky wasn't the only team member who had experience in the intelligence field, Charlie Dawkins had extensive experience with the State

Department, and he, too, had proven himself under fire in Alaska, the Amazon, and Iraq. Brad picked up his BlackBerry and speed-dialed Charlie's BlackBerry.

Charlie Dawkins, a rawboned six footer with coal-black hair, deep blue eyes, and big hands, had spent years in the clandestine service of the Department of State. Team Dallas had first encountered Charlie in Alaska in a confrontation with Lewis Hostback and the Order of Phineas. Charlie and Brad's cousin Jessica had become close—that was inaccurate, they had become lovers, something Brad understood but was still a little uneasy about. His memories of his svelte, golden-haired cousin extended back to the days when she had just started kindergarten and was small enough to bounce on his knee. The notion of her sleeping with anyone, not just Charlie Dawkins, made his skin crawl.

Jessica, however, had been adventurous and bold all her life and most definitely had a mind of her own. Her father, Brad's Uncle Jack, was wealthy in his own right and would have given Jessica anything, but Jessica had turned treasure hunter for the adventure of it and to seek a fortune of her own. She had become caught up in the thrill of what Brad was doing when she wheeled her way onto the Alaska mission. She had proved to be a natural and had earned her spurs with her athleticism, her marksmanship, and her ruthlessness in action.

"Charlie?"

"Hey Brad, we were just talking about you."

"All good, I hope."

"Jess just caught a news bulletin about a Bill Duckworth being abducted in Brunei. She mentioned that she had met him at your Uncle

Jack's house, and then we wondered together if Team Dallas was going to get involved in it..."

"We are, and I'm calling to see if you're familiar with Borneo or the *Jemaah Islamiyah.* We'll be going wheels up within the next twenty-four hours, and I need as much help as I can get assimilating all the information I've gathered ... and it would be a big help to talk to someone who's been there. Do you have any old contacts at State who've had boots on the ground anywhere near Borneo?"

"Don't need any, Brad, I spent over a year there with a Ghurka battalion because of the cross-border attacks from *Abu Sayyaf.* My knowledge is a couple of years out of date, but what I do have is firsthand instead of just from books."

"Charlie, that's the best news I've heard all day! How soon can you get over here?"

"On my way, Brad!"

Scott Conrad

*   *   *

Brad got up to start a pot of coffee for the brainstorming session. While he busied his hands with the task, his mind was engaged in deciding the best way to reorganize the warehouse to make it easier to access the equipment that Vicky and Willona were cataloging. Willona was right about that, too, in more ways than she knew. Looking back over the years, Brad could see how much time he had wasted shopping around for equipment or weapons before each mission.

For the first time he thought seriously about Willona's recommendation that he consider moving someplace where he could have everything under one roof. He and Vicky had not discussed their future openly yet, but the time was coming for that decision as well. The possibility of having a permanent relationship with her had a certain appeal, but the idea of living in a home office no longer seemed like such a great idea.

Willona and Ving seemed to have a much fuller life than he had managed so far. Perhaps he should consider converting a portion of the warehouse… That idea died aborning. The warehouse was too small, and the drive to it would take too long. He sighed. Perhaps the smartest thing to do would be to wait for Willona's suggestions.

FOUR

"Hi Brad! Coffee ready?" Jessica Paul led Charlie Dawkins into Brad's apartment without bothering to knock. Brad, lounging in his recliner with his laptop computer open and a steaming mug of dark roast coffee in one hand, set everything down on his coffee table and stood up.

"Jess, Charlie, glad you could get here so quickly." He gave his cousin a hug and shook hands with Charlie. He hadn't expected Jessica, but he realized he should have. The two seemed to be joined at the hip nowadays ... where you saw one, you invariably saw the other. "Charlie, we're pressed for time so I'm going to give you a summary of the situation as I understand it right now. We've been given the mission of repatriating William Darnell Duckworth IV, CEO of Duckworth International Petroleum. Duckworth was taken by members of Jemaah Islamiyah after leaving Brunei International Airport in Bandar Seri Begawan ...

snatched him right out of his chauffeur driven limo." Brad paused for a moment then continued.

"Duckworth International has an intelligence committee made up of former members of the C.I.A., most of who are lawyers. The director of this committee is a guy named Grainger. He told me his team has determined that Duckworth has been taken to an unknown location in South Kalimantan, the Indonesian southern part of the island of Borneo. Apparently the jihadists failed to inactivate Duckworth's satellite phone until after he'd been captive for several hours. The JI has been in contact with the committee, but negotiations have stalled. The consensus of the committee is that the kidnappers seem more interested in making a political statement than in collecting the ransom money." Brad spread his arms wide, palms up. "In a nutshell, that's all I've got, and I'm hoping you can add to that, Charlie."

Charlie cocked his head to one side and pursed his lips, thinking for a moment before speaking.

"I'll get us some coffee, Charlie," Jessica said, heading for the coffee pot. She called back over her shoulder. "Brad, dining room table or your office?"

"Office," Brad said. He led the way back to his office, once again thinking that he needed more space, but his computers and reference materials were in there; the laptop's screen was just too small to share between three people. He beckoned Charlie toward one of the leather wingback chairs beside his desk, and Charlie took a seat.

"I've been all over Borneo, Brad. Do you remember the troubles with Abu Sayyaf in the '90s?"

Brad nodded. Abu Sayyaf had been listed as a terrorist group by the U.S. Department of State after it was launched in the early 1990s in the Philippine province of Basilan, roughly a hundred miles northeast of Sulu Province. The radical

Islamist group set up its headquarters on Jolo Island and quickly became widely known for its raids, its kidnappings for ransom, and its beheadings.

"The State Department sent a single agent to Brunei at the Sultan's request to keep track of Abu Sayyaf's activities, but in the early 2000s, Jemaah Islamiyah, which had been drawing revenues from al-Qaeda, began to rapidly expand their overt operations. The State Department had been keeping an eye on them because of their indirect involvement in the '93 World Trade Center bombing and the unsuccessful 'Bojinka' plot, but when they began to escalate, State sent a second agent to Brunei and opened a small field office there. In 2014, Abu Bakar Bashir swore allegiance to ISIL while in the maximum-security *Pasir Putih* prison in Nusakambangan, an island near the coast of Cilacap, Central Java, and called for all members of JI to do the same. The Department of State countered by adding another agent to the field office in Bandar Seri Begawan—me."

"So you were actually stationed in Brunei?"

"Yes, but I spent very little time in the Sultanate. My job was to follow the Army and investigators from the *Polis Diraja Brunei* (Royal Brunei Police Force) to the JI crime scenes all over the island of Borneo. I've been 'boots on the ground' in Brunei, Sarawak, and all of Kalimantan."

Brad's fingers fairly flew over the keyboard to his desktop workstation, pulling up a map of the island of Borneo, converting it from a map to a satellite image and directing it to a sixty-inch color television monitor on the wall.

"Show me."

Charlie stood and walked to the monitor, using his finger to indicate spots he had been to and relating the incidents that had spurred his visits. The list was long, and Jessica listened wide-eyed, hearing about this part of Charlie's life for the first time.

Brad stared at the map.

"Grainger said his committee lost the signal from Duckworth's phone in a town called Muara Teweh, Charlie. Show me where that's at."

Charlie's finger went to a spot in Central Kalimantan, roughly a hundred and twenty miles from the eastern coast of the island as the crow flies.

"Mantiqi III!" Charlie said triumphantly.

"Huh?"

"Mantiqi III," Charlie repeated. "JI's ... I guess you could call it their training division for lack of a better term. Part of it's located down here, in South Kalimantan." He pointed to a mountainous area on the map about forty miles inland from the coastal city of Sebamban. "There are valleys all through these mountains, filled with some of the most rotten, miserable rainforests you've ever seen."

"Worse than the Congo?" Jessica asked, a skeptical expression on her face.

"No place is worse than the Congo," Brad retorted drily.

"I've never seen the Congo, but it's hard for me to imagine anything worse than what I encountered in South Kalimantan. The Indonesian Army refuses to enter that particular area, and the government doesn't permit overflights by Brunei ... or anyone else for that matter. I managed to penetrate to within a hundred meters of Mantiqi III's location and I've seen it with my own eyes."

Brad's eyebrows raised slightly in question.

"The Indonesian government has made a special effort to cooperate with foreign governments in the arrest and prosecution of terrorists, but it's a majority Muslim country and in some parts of it there is a great deal of public sympathy for Islamic militants." His finger tapped the mountainous area firmly several times. "This is one of those areas. I've been told by reliable sources that JI has a relatively permanent training base in this area and a permanent cadre of about twenty guys ... and that is augmented by volunteers when they have a large recruit class." Charlie stopped for a moment, as if making up his mind about something, and then shook his head.

"On June 30, 2003, in response to the 2002 Bali bombings, the Indonesian National Police formed a special forces type counter-terrorism squad. It is funded, equipped, and trained by the U.S. and Australia. The squad's official name is Special Detachment 88 (*Detasemen Khusus 88*), but it is also known as Delta 88 or Densus 88. This special unit receives funding from the U.S. government channeled through the Department of State's Diplomatic Security Service (DSS), my former employer. The unit gets its training from C.I.A., F.B.I., and U.S. Secret Service personnel at a classified facility in Megamendung, about fifty klicks south of Jakarta.

"From time to time, Detachment 88 requests—and receives—assistance from specialists working for foreign governments on joint operations. On a number of occasions involving ongoing investigations of Jemaah Islamiyah I was one of those specialists. I worked with a special agent of Detachment 88 named Daniel Novianti and we became close friends. It was Daniel who showed me the way to Camp Bashir, named after the cleric who founded Jemaah Islamiyah."

A look of pained indecision passed over Charlie's face, and then he seemed to come to a decision. "The camp is still in operation and quietly sheltered by the Indonesian National Police (INP) because there is an ongoing deep cover operation going on there. They have a guy inside JI and he is very successfully feeding them vital information on some al-Qaeda bomb making experts who are alleged to be engaged in making a dirty bomb with cesium. They don't want this op exposed, and if they figure out we're trying to go in there, they'll do everything they can to stop us."

"Even if it means Duckworth gets his head chopped off?" Brad was pissed. If the INP had a guy inside and knew the identity of the bomb makers, they had enough information to take the camp out. The odor of politics was strong in his nostrils and it stank to high heaven.

"There's more going on here than just getting some ransom money, Brad. I don't know for certain just what it is, but it's not just about the money."

"That's pretty much what Grainger said was his 'committee's' conclusion. He said they told him that JI planned to execute Duckworth whether they collect the ransom money or not."

Jessica looked up at her cousin in alarm.

"Then why aren't we moving already?

"Because something about this stinks, Jess ... and because we don't commit to this type of operation any more until we've done our homework. I'm tired of bringing my team home full of holes and wondering if I might have done a better job of protecting them if I'd done my homework better," Brad said grimly. "There's no way to guarantee that no one will get hurt—or worse—on a mission, I know that. I also know that the better you prepare the better your chances of coming out in one piece. I've been running a knee-jerk, seat-of-the-pants operation for years, and I've decided to put a screeching halt to that. I can't eliminate the 'crisis' nature of this business, but I can and will initiate an alert sequence that permits us to better prepare for our missions. It's all in the works right now. Willona is putting everything together for my approval, and I'm hoping she'll have a business plan completed by the time we finish this mission."

Charlie was nodding his head in silent approval, but Jessica still looked skeptical.

"Even in the Corps, Jess, we had an alert sequence when activating a unit ... and that was only initiated after a great deal of intelligence and research had been gathered and analyzed. The military has a huge support staff and virtually limitless resources far more than we have. At the same time, we have access to technology that simply wasn't available just a few years ago. Instant communications, GPS, global mapping technology and research via the internet, thermal imaging, drones ... the list is endless, and it all helps us to do our job better and more efficiently. Some of this stuff is so new that I never had it in the Corps. It would have made a hell of a difference, and I can think of a lot of comrades who would still be here today if we'd had it."

* * *

Vicky sat down on a pallet holding the folded up canvas of an Army surplus G.P. Medium tent and mopped her forehead with a large, blue bandana. A clipboard lay on the floor between her feet, a yellow legal pad held in its metal clasp, and a mechanical pencil lay atop the pad. Several pages of the pad were filled with descriptions and tallies of equipment and supplies.

"How in the hell does he manage to find anything in here?" she asked.

Willona Ving, dressed in jeans and sneakers, her own bandana tied around her head '60s style, was scribbling furiously on her own clipboard.

"Child, I have no idea. It's no wonder he spends so much money duplicating things. He has equipment stacked everywhere and there doesn't seem to be any rhyme or reason to it at all."

"At least it's clean," Vicky remarked.

"I expected it to be, I just didn't expect everything to be scattered around like this. What were they thinking?" Willona was shaking her head as she looked around the two-thousand-square-foot warehouse. "Even with better shelving and a forklift to lift stuff and move it around there's not enough room for all this gear. Even when we consolidate it and remove the redundancies, he's going to need more room."

"I'm sure that it was empty when he bought it. It must have seemed huge to him then," Vicky said. "What do you have in mind, Willona?"

"I don't know for sure," Willona said, chewing on the eraser end of her yellow number 2 pencil. "I have some friends in real estate that I can check with. We need an appraisal on this place that's certain. Brad got a really good deal on this when he bought it, and commercial property values have skyrocketed around Dallas/Fort Worth in the last few years. The smart thing to do would be to find a ranchette with some good outbuildings and enough room to build a decent warehouse. The problem with that is finding one near the metropolitan area for anything resembling any kind of affordable price anymore."

"I don't know much about real estate prices around here, Willona. Is it really that bad?"

"High to mid seven figures minimum."

"Jesus, can Brad afford that?" She really didn't have any idea of what Brad Jacobs was worth, had never even thought about it.

Willona scratched her scalp with the yellow pencil.

"Depends. I'm not sure what I can get for this place and his apartment—he owns that, by the way. If I can find a ranchette going for back taxes or in a distress sale, I might be able to work some kind of deal. The trick is going to be working a deal that gives him … us … enough left over to make whatever improvements are necessary to adapt the place to fit the company's needs."

FIVE

TARAKAN CITY, NORTH KALIMANTAN, INDONESIA, SEPTEMBER 28, 2010

The mood in the city was ugly. The Tidung, a Dayak tribe native to the island of Tarakan, already angry with the immigrant Bugis, whom they felt were taking their jobs and receiving preferential treatment from the government, were furious over an incident the day before. A man called Abdullah, a Tidung civic and spiritual leader from northern Tarakan, had been killed while trying to exact revenge against a gang of young immigrant men who had thrashed his son. The youths were *Bugis Letta*, an ethnic sub-group of the Bugis people who had originally moved to Tarakan from South Sulawesi's Pinrang District as part of the official Indonesian transmigration policy. The fighting was bloody and many of the Bugis were fleeing, putting an enormous strain on the city's resources.

The Central Command of the governing council of Jemaah Islamiyah had pounced on the opportunity unfolding in Tarakan to broaden the rift between the indigenous Tidung and the immigrant Bugis. Even though the Bugis were predominantly Muslim, a confrontation between any of the Dayak sects and immigrants would be like pouring gasoline on the simmering flames of resentment Jemaah Islamiyah had been fanning for years. The internal strife was the key element of the JI strategy to bring down the governments and establish a caliphate encompassing the entire island of Borneo. The Council sent a coded message to Mantiqi II.

Bintang Fadlhan, the senior commander in Mantiqi II assigned to the Tarakan City wakalah, had sent an urgent request for Amir Ibrahim because of his reputation for expertise with explosives, and Ibrahim had been flown to the city from the mainland in a black helicopter flown by two Americans. There had been another American aboard the flight, a man wearing an expensive, hand-tailored, blue suit, a white shirt, a black tie, and aviator sunglasses. The man carried a slim leather briefcase, and he never said a word. Ibrahim was very uncomfortable being transported by agents of The Great Satan, but Fadlhan had reassured him that these particular Americans were not the enemy. Ibrahim did not speak to any of the three, and he kept his rifle loaded and off safe during the entire trip.

* * *

Dressed in civilian street clothes—jeans, a tee shirt, and a hat pulled low over his eyes to disguise his face—Amir Ibrahim crouched down in the lee of a damaged retaining wall, placing one of his radio detonated incendiary devices into the foundation of a private residence. He had built the devices in the privacy of a safe house Jemaah Islamiyah maintained in the very shadow of the Masjid Al Maarif Mosque in the eastern part of the city near the port. Despite the reassurances he had been given that the sacrifice was a necessary one, Amir felt a tug at his conscience as he placed the device on the home of yet another Muslim.

"Are your other charges placed and primed?" Ibrahim glanced up to see the grim face of a man he knew only as Khalil. He had worked alongside Khalil in Syria and knew him to be a more than competent combat leader and an absolute demon at hand-to-hand combat, which he realized was probably why Fadlhan had selected him to lead this mission. The Bugis were not heavily armed, nor were the Tidung. The JI team was armed only with weapons common to the two groups—the Dayak Mandau, the parang, the blowpipes tipped with spearheads, the wicked looking Kris of the Bugis. The only modern weapons they carried were the 9mm semi-automatic pistols, which they had been ordered to conceal and to dispose of if there was the slightest chance they might be captured by the police or by the government troops that had been sent in. Even Ibrahim's remote detonator was installed in the case of a cheap throwaway flip phone.

"Yes," Ibrahim answered. "All is in readiness, this is the last one. I can set them off singly at your command according to the plan or I can set them off all at once."

"Good! Let's get up with the others and get started. The rest of the team should be gathered by the hotel on the waterfront. Halim says a good-sized group of Tidung is on the way there looking for the gang that killed Abdullah."

"I have no idea whether any of my devices will be near that group," Ibrahim protested.

"You placed them at the locations marked on the maps I gave you?" Khalil snapped.

"Yes, of course."

"Then do not concern yourself. We have team elements in place that will ensure the Bugis will believe the Tidung set the fires. Do you have your kris?" Khalil had issued the vicious looking kris, famous for their wavy blades, to all members of the insurgent team when they had first gathered in a warehouse near the airport as he had explained their mission and issued their original assignments.

Khalil glanced down at his own cellphone, first checking the time and then checking his text messages to see if all his elements were in place. When he was satisfied that all was in order, he waved for Ibrahim to follow him. "I want to see the first few go up," he said through tight lips.

* * *

The explosion was not loud at all, but the shooting flames were spectacular, and they quickly enveloped the small, neat house. A woman in flames carrying an infant child in her arms ran screaming from the front door, and Ibrahim could hear other voices inside the inferno shrieking in agony. Ibrahim's guts knotted up with guilt over the cruelty of his own actions, but he quickly fought the feelings down. Fadlhan had explained in great detail that while there would be individual injustices and great sorrow, their actions were an absolutely necessary element to the establishment of the caliphate, which the Prophet, peace be unto him, had commanded them to build.

A small crowd of onlookers, young Tidung wearing Mandau swords in their sashes, hooted gleefully at the sight of the burning woman and raised their fists and their voices as neighbors of the Bugis family poured out into the yard trying hopelessly to put out the fire. As soon as the mood of the neighbors turned ugly, Khalil tugged at Ibrahim's sleeve and they melted away down the block, making for the site of the next device, several blocks away.

*   *   *

The group of Tidung in front of the next site had not waited for the detonation; they were already taunting the residents and shouting insulting epithets at the angry neighbors. Another member of Khalil's team of instigators had joined with them as they approached the second site, dressed in traditional Bugis garb. At a nod from Khalil, the new man broke away and made his way toward the Tidung agitators.

"Now!" Khalil hissed at Ibrahim.

Saying a silent prayer asking forgiveness, Ibrahim closed his eyes and pressed the next button in the sequence, setting off the incendiary device he had placed an hour before. Despite his misgivings about building the devices, his skill hadn't flagged. There was a loud bang and flames began to lick the walls of the residence, spreading with amazing speed because of the liquid accelerant he had incorporated into the devices. The effect was so spectacular that Ibrahim almost missed the deliberate murder of one of Khalil's instigators ... by the team member that had just joined them in the street. It was all he could do to maintain his calm as he watched the new man plunge a kris, a clearly recognizable symbol of the Bugis, into the belly of one of the agitators and begin to curse the Tidung agitators loudly in Buginese.

The crowd of neighbors, stunned at first by the blast and the flames, hesitated only a moment before their mood turned ugly. The Tidung, incensed by the stabbing of one of their own, unsheathed their Mandau swords and surged toward the Bugis residents. Unlike the Madurese immigrants the paid agitators had been harrying throughout Kalimantan over the past few years, the Bugis were less susceptible to intimidation, and soon there was a full-fledged melee around the burning home. The anguished occupants of the house seemed to have been forgotten by the mob. Khalil, satisfied that all had gone according to his plan, nudged the astonished Ibrahim and began to walk discreetly toward the third site, a small satisfied smirk on his dark face.

*　*　*

By the time they reached the fourth site, large numbers of the native Tidung were roaming the streets, searching for the killers of Abdullah and menacing the immigrant Bugis at every turn. The fighting was beginning to get bloody, and the streets were filled with fleeing Bugis families frightened by the hordes of angry Tidung. Ibrahim could see smoke rising from dwellings and buildings in every direction from fires that he had not set.

"Set the rest of them off now," Khalil growled. "We have work to do elsewhere." He turned without waiting for Ibrahim's response and began to make his way toward the waterfront hotel where the rest of the team was waiting.

Ibrahim had just flipped open the cheap cell phone to press the appropriate buttons when he was blindsided and knocked sprawling to the pavement. He got to his knees, shaking his head to clear it and wiping his skinned palms on his cotton trousers. The man who had knocked him down was one of the paid agitators from the second site, and he was mad as hell. The agitator had fire in his eyes as he crouched, Mandau sword weaving a hypnotic dance in his hand as he hissed at Khalil.

"You set us up!" he rasped.

Ibrahim had seen Khalil fight before, and he recognized the leader's subtle shift into a fighting stance. The agitator had no idea that his own life was about to be forfeit.

"It was the will of Allah," Khalil said with false gentleness.

"It was not the will of Allah, you bastard, it was your will!" The agitator danced around looking for an opening, but Khalil continued to shift almost imperceptibly, his dark eyes locked on the wrists of the agitator—it was the wrists that would warn him of the impending sword strike.

With no further warning the agitator raised the Mandau above his head in both hands and began his lunge toward Khalil. It was only then that Ibrahim realized he had withdrawn the kris that Khalil had given him from the folds of his loose cotton shirt. He did not stop to think, he simply stepped forward and plunged the kris into the agitator's back, the crooked point slipping up from beneath the man's ribcage and penetrating his heart. The agitator was dead before his body hit the ground, but Ibrahim's precipitous action had been observed by the Tidung and they immediately mobbed him, kicking and pummeling him mercilessly. Khalil simply faded into the background and, unnoticed, slipped away. Ibrahim was on his own, and fighting the murderous crowd for his life.

A rough, calloused foot caught him beneath the chin and Ibrahim went down again, blood pouring from his nose and ears. He rolled over onto his belly and spat bits of a broken tooth out onto the rough pavement as he protected his head as best he could with his bruised and battered hands. Another well-placed kick caught him in the kidney and he rolled over onto his back, the mob still screaming and cursing at him. Several participants in the mob were brandishing their headhunter's Mandau swords menacingly and Ibrahim knew that it was time to take drastic action. The hard metal of the Beretta 92F Khalil had given him earlier pressed painfully into his back … he had forgotten it was there.

Ibrahim scrabbled wildly for the gun butt and finally felt his fingers curl around it well enough to tug it out. His thumb flicked the safety lever off and he began firing wildly as soon as the barrel cleared the waistband of his trousers. He didn't really intend to kill anyone; he just wanted to clear the mob from around him long enough to get away from them. After a half dozen wild shots the mob fled, leaving three bleeding bodies in the street. Ibrahim didn't even check to see if his victims were alive or dead, he simply ran for the closest alley and faded into the dark underbelly of the city.

* * *

There were cuts on his face, and he thought his nose might be broken, but he could still walk. As he limped painfully down back streets towards the hotel rally point, avoiding the angry roaming crowds, Amir Ibrahim had time to reflect on the increasingly uncomfortable nature of this "hurry up" mission. Fadlhan's reassurances rang hollow in his ears after observing the Tidung and the Bugis in Tarakan. He had fought and trained in Syria, Iraq, and Afghanistan, paying close attention to the logic, strategic planning, and mission execution of the leaders appointed over him. Tarakan was not large enough or of sufficient economic significance to warrant the kind of strategy being employed in this mission. Never, in all the years Ibrahim had been involved with Jemaah Islamiyah, had he known the organization to pit Muslim against Muslim.

The participation of the Americans in the operation added to his worries, and the only conclusion he was able to come to was that Fadlhan might be up to some stratagem of his own devising, a startling thought that did nothing to ease Ibrahim's concerns. He forced himself to suppress his suspicions, telling himself that the JI leadership would never allow the cause to be tainted and that they were wiser than he. He succeeded in burying his misgivings in Fadlhan, but his resentment of Khalil boiled to the surface.

Ibrahim understood that Khalil's primary concern had to be the mission, but the man's callous and deliberate cold-blooded sacrifice of the agitator at the site of the second detonation and his coldhearted abandonment of Ibrahim to the angry Tidung mob was gnawing at his guts. Ibrahim did not see his own unthinking execution of the paid agitator in the same light, as his purpose had been to spare the life of the leader and ensure the successful completion of the mission. Even so, the entire mission remained extremely unsettling to Ibrahim because its purpose was to set Muslim against Muslim.

Grimacing against the aches and pains from his beating, Ibrahim continued making his way toward the hotel. Except for Khalil and his team, he was alone in Tarakan. Despite his increasing dislike for the man, Khalil held his reputation with the rest of the JI leadership in the palm of his hand. The only thing to do was to satisfy Khalil and get as far away from Tarakan as he could just as quickly as he could. It was a small enough price to pay to get back to his real work, his holy cause. When he was finished with whatever Fadlhan had lured him into, he would take responsibility for the consequences of his actions and make atonement (*kafara*) for them so that Allah would grant him forgiveness (*ghufran*).

* * *

Lawrence P. Waldingham III shot the cuffs of his tailored Egyptian cotton shirt and checked the creases of his trousers before checking the positioning of his bodyguards and sitting down at the wrought-iron table across from Bintang Fadlhan. The table was under an awning at a sidewalk café in one of the more upscale business districts of Tarakan City. The two men calmly watched the cordon of police in full riot gear that separated the business from the angry mobs in the street.

"I'm not sure that meeting in such a public place was wise," Waldingham said in a low voice.

Fadlhan calmly reached for a delicate china teacup from the tray in front of him and began an elaborate preparation ritual that Waldingham had seen before.

"I have told you before, Lawrence, Tarakan City belongs to me," he said, setting five cubes of sugar in the bottom of the cup. Then he selected some loose tea leaves from a silver salver on the serving tray and placed them in the cup atop the sugar cubes. With a delicacy and grace that belied his size, Fadlhan lifted the teapot and poured steaming hot water into the cup. "I needed Ibrahim's particular skill set and you provided the fastest means of getting him here."

"I understand, but do you really think it was necessary for us to meet in public? Is that wise?"

Fadlhan set the teapot down abruptly and leaned forward, his serene features twisting into a more menacing conformation.

"I told you this is a safe place for us, Lawrence. Your continued doubt in my veracity makes me wonder if I may have been in error when I selected you as a partner in my little venture."

"Taking over a country is hardly what I would describe as a 'little venture', Fadlhan. It's a risky business and I have no desire to be stood in front of a brick wall and executed … or beheaded. Your followers seem to prefer the latter method," Wallingham said sourly, not intimidated.

"You are being paid well to take the risks, Lawrence, and when my plan comes to fruition, the payoff will be spectacular and you know it," Fadlhan said evenly.

"It had better be. If it fails there will be consequences, I can promise you that." Waldingham was keeping a file of Fadlhan's activities under the guise of a covert operation. There was only one copy, and it had not been committed to a computer file. Fifteen years' clandestine service with the C.I.A. had taught him that no computer could keep a secret from a determined hacker, and both the Company and N.S.A. had the best hackers in the world. He was only willing to risk his government pension on his own terms, and the risks were paltry compared to the billion or so dollars he was assured of if Fadlhan's scheme worked out. In the meantime, he would be at the beck and call of this supercilious revolutionary, and that would require patience and the avoidance of obvious stupidities. He sighed, putting on a false smile.

"I'm sorry, Fadlhan. I haven't slept well lately and it has obviously taken a toll on my patience."

"Very well, Lawrence, but in future it would be best if you didn't call my judgment into question." Somewhat mollified, Fadlhan lifted his teacup and sipped at it as his eyes roved approvingly over the angry rioting mob in the street.

SIX

Team Dallas was assembled around the table in Brad's living room, and once again Brad was reminded of just how inadequate his apartment was for Team business. There was, however, nothing that could be done about it at the moment.

He looked around the table. Vicky, Ving, Willona, Charlie, and Jessica were to his left, and to his right were Pete Sabrowski and Jared Smoot. Pete was a great grizzled bear of a man and could fly anything that could get off the ground. The taciturn Jared Smoot looked like a typical Texas cowhand, but he was the finest sniper Brad had ever encountered. Both men had served with Brad in Force Recon.

Only Jessica and Charlie had heard all the details so far. It was Brad's intention to let Charlie give the initial mission briefing since he was the only team member who had actually been on the ground in Borneo and was better prepared to answer questions. Brad pressed some keys on his laptop, sending the map on its screen to the big screen television he'd moved to the dining room from its regular spot in the living room.

"Ain't technology grand?" Jared drawled, sipping from a white china coffee mug. Everyone else was drinking coffee, but the lanky sniper was sipping his favorite beverage, hot chocolate prepared from the contents of the pouch that he carried with him everywhere he went. He had never revealed the recipe to anyone except Vicky as far as Brad knew. Brad cleared his throat and the members of Team Dallas looked to him expectantly.

"I have accepted a mission contract. William Duckworth of Duckworth International Petroleum was abducted by members of Jemaah Islamiyah day before yesterday. DIP's intelligence committee tracked him as far as Muara Teweh in Central Kalimantan, Indonesia, on the island of Borneo. Charlie here has worked and traveled extensively on the island and is familiar with both Jemaah Islamiyah and the territory, so he's going to be giving the initial briefing. Charlie?"

The first part of the briefing was a thorough rehash of the abduction from the start through to the committee losing track of Duckworth. The second part of the briefing was a description of the terrain and the Indonesian government.

"I have an active contact in the Intelligence Detachment of *Gegana*, which in turn is part of the Mobile Brigade Corps (*Korps Brigade Mobil*, abbreviated BRIMOB), a special operations/paramilitary unit inside the Indonesian National Police Force (POLRI). Its primary duties include counter-terrorism, riot control, high-risk law enforcement where the use of firearms is likely, search and rescue, hostage rescue, and explosive ordnance disposal ops.

"My contact is a guy named Daniel, and he has been shadowing Jemaah Islamiyah since 1995. Not only have I worked with the guy on the ground in Kalimantan, I have actually seen the compound where we are ninety percent certain that Duckworth is being held." Everyone sat up straighter at this point, listening hard.

"Daniel and I have stayed in touch for the last few years since I left Brunei. While we were waiting for everyone to get here, I spent some time on the phone with him. Daniel has confirmed that Duckworth is being held at the Camp Bashir training center.

"*Gegana* has a deep cover asset inside the training center and the Indonesian National Police are flatly refusing to compromise him. Daniel says, off the record of course, that he is willing to funnel information to me, but he emphasized that the INP absolutely will not take an active role in the repatriation ... quite the opposite. If we're caught bringing weapons into the country, or even caught with weapons in our possession while we are there, we will be incarcerated and punished to the fullest extent of the law.

"The government of Indonesia has been ultra-cooperative with other nations in the pursuit and punishment of radical Islamists, but they jealously guard their sovereignty and somebody high up in the government is hot for the current head of JI. No matter what happens, we can't expect them to help us or even cut us any slack."

"So we're basically screwed?" Pete asked.

"JI killed a couple of cops out of *Gegana's* CBR Detachment, and the Intelligence Detachment has reason to believe that the shooter's brother is part of the cadre at the training center. They want the shooter bad; consider it a matter of honor to apprehend him. There is also reason to believe that the shooter has information that will lead to the location of the guy who's been trying to build a dirty bomb with some stolen cesium. There's no chance we're going to get any overt assistance whatsoever. There is good news though. Daniel has agreed to put me in contact with a black market arms dealer who can provide anything we need for the mission, so we won't get caught trying to sneak weapons into the country."

"That'll be a great comfort to me when they lock me up and throw away the key for totin' guns in the jungle," Pete muttered.

"Not to worry 'bout getting' locked up, Pete," Jared drawled, sipping once more at his hot chocolate, "they don't lock you up in Indonesia for breakin' the law—Sharia Law by the way—they just whip out a machete and make ya a foot shorter."

Uneasy laughter swept around the table.

Brad spoke up, his face set in a neutral expression.

"I've never done this before," he said, glancing down at his hands, "but I find myself considering things I never have before when prepping for a mission." He looked at Ving and Willona first, then

Vicky, before meeting the eyes of the rest of Team Dallas one at a time. "This mission is different."

"You having second thoughts, Brad?" Ving asked, concern evident on his broad face. The same concern was plain on every face in the room.

"Not for myself. I'm concerned that the rest of you don't understand what we are facing here. A nation ruled by the tenets of Sharia Law. A government trapped between its own laws and its desire to cooperate with the international community in catching and punishing Islamic militants, and a public that is, if not largely sympathetic to the insurgents, then inclined to look the other way. In short, a one hundred percent hostile environment going in and coming out, with the very real threat of the legitimate government coming after us. You do realize that there is only one punishment for lawbreakers under Sharia Law?"

There was absolute silence in the room as the team pondered his words. After several minutes of uncomfortable silence, Ving was the one who broke the ice.

"Aw hell, Brad, for a minute there I thought you was gonna tell me I couldn't carry none of Willona's bacon sammiches with me cuz we'd be goin' into a Muslim country. I'm gone tell you right now, makin' no bones about it … if I can't take my bacon sammiches I ain't goin'." Ving tried to maintain a straight face throughout his brief monologue, but by the end he was grinning widely. As always when he was clowning, his New Orleans accent came out thick and exaggerated. The rest of the team broke out in laughter.

Jared managed to keep his face straight through the general hilarity.

"I ain't studyin' 'bout no sammiches," he drawled. "Don't reckon them folks gonna care one way or the other 'bout my cocoa. I'm in. Brad." There were snickers from the others because Jared Smoot's drawl got worse when he was clowning too.

Pete Sabrowski put his two cents worth in next, only he wasn't trying to be funny.

"I'm trying not to be offended, Brad. We've most of us been together for a long time, some bad places and some tight spots. We've lost friends and comrades in circumstances no sane person should have had to be put in, and never once has any of us failed to toe the line. I know the words "Semper Fi" mean as much to you as they do to the rest of us. This is just another mission to me, brother. I'm in." The others nodded in approval.

Brad felt foolish even as a surge of pride ran through him. The doubts he had felt moments before shamed him a little even though he had to acknowledge that they were legitimate concerns. What he had forgotten was the old adage that was the mantra of the Corps as expressed by a popular television reality show star—improvise, adapt, overcome. His team hadn't forgotten what it meant, and he shouldn't have either.

*   *   *

Half an hour later, after a tight-lipped and unhappy Willona had made a second pot of coffee and Jared had carefully prepared a second cup of his special cocoa, the team settled into a sober discussion, brainstorming the best approach to the mission. Pete Sabrowski, the fly anything aviator, wondered aloud whether a seaplane would be the best option for the infiltration into Kalimantan.

"I dunno, Pete, lookin' at that map I'm thinkin' the best way to get in there undetected is a HALO (High Altitude Low Opening) insertion." It pained him to even make the suggestion; Brad knew Ving hated even the idea of jumping out of a perfectly good aircraft more than anything.

"You're probably right," Ving replied, "but I'm thinking it's gonna be just as important to get outta there in a hurry as it is to get in there in a hurry."

"And we've got forty or more miles to negotiate before we can reach even the closest seacoast," Vicky added.

Jared spoke up. "Polaris manufactures an incredibly versatile all-terrain vehicle that's both compact and capable of carrying either six people or two people and up to 1500 pounds of equipment; the Corps has adopted a version of it to accelerate the rapid deployment of infantry troops in terrain where jeeps and other ATVs just won't go. Why don't you pull up a picture of it on your internet and see what you think?"

Brad didn't hesitate. "What am I looking for?"

"Polaris MRZR-D4," Jared responded.

Brad keyed in the term and punched "Enter", and an image popped up on screen.

"Hmmm, looks good," Brad mused. "4-Stroke Three Cylinder Turbo Diesel, 2100 pounds, twelve-inch ground clearance, cargo box, on demand four-wheel drive, a hundred and seven inch wheelbase, fifty inches wide…" He glanced up at Pete. "Do you think it's air transportable or is that too big for a small aircraft?"

Pete shrugged. "Depends on what kind of bird we use, Brad. Aside from that, I'd really need to take a look at one close up before I could say for sure."

Brad picked up the handset to his landline and read the phone number for the local dealership off the webpage then punched in the number.

"Hi. My name is Jacobs and I need to know if you can arrange a demo for me and a few of my friends…"

* * *

"You might be interested to know that our military people love this model. It has been adopted by the Army and the Marine Corps and unofficially dubbed the 'Mrazor'. I guess the military penchant for acronyms spurs these odd nicknames."

The team was delighted with the vehicle. Each of them put it through its paces, reveling in its power and agility and especially its relative quiet.

Pete looked the twelve-foot-long vehicle over for almost an hour, talking with the salesman and asking question after question. When he was satisfied, he turned to Brad.

"She's air transportable all right, if we can find the right aircraft. It would be better if we could use a Caribou, but I didn't see any place we could land one anywhere near there ... even if we could find one in Indonesia." The Caribou, known in the military as a C7A, was a military aircraft with a short takeoff and landing capability that had in large part been retired from military service. Not that many had been manufactured and the attrition rate had been high. Finding one available in Indonesia or anywhere in that part of the world would be unlikely.

"I've been thinking about it," Brad said. "A seaplane is going to be our best bet. We need to get in without being noticed, and the coast is going to be our best bet."

"That works best for the drug smugglers too," Charlie remarked drily.

Brad shrugged.

"There's a reason for that, Charlie. If you're met by the INP or the Indonesian equivalent of the Coast Guard, turning around and flying out is a better option than slugging it out with a better armed and better prepared opponent." He turned to Willona. "The price on these is pretty stout at thirty-six grand; can we afford one of them?"

She gave him a wry look. "I'm going against my better judgment, which, by the way, is that all of you are insane for even considering this mission, but I prepared a provisional budget for this mission and then tripled it to determine the amount of the retainer. If you're resolved to take this on, you should probably buy two of them. You're going to have seven people and whatever equipment you're carrying with you, and that thing won't carry more than six people. Besides, I'm counting on you bringing them back so we can depreciate them over a period of years. In case you didn't know it, we can write that off on your taxes."

She bunched her fists and put them on her hips. "You can buy them. But you'd better be damned sure you bring them back, though, and my crazy ass husband with them. Leaving them behind is not an option, they are not disposables." She faced away from him for a moment to glare at Ving and then turned back to Brad again. "And don't go tearing them up either!"

"Two questions: First, are there any Polaris dealerships in Indonesia? Second, if there are, can

I buy them through you and take possession there so I don't have to pay for transporting them over there?" Brad asked the salesman.

"I'll have to check, but I'm sure we'll be able to work something out." The salesman, eager to make a double sale, especially one where he didn't have to do anything but take the money and hand some paperwork over to his clerk, was practically drooling. "Come on inside and let's take a look." He rushed toward his office without waiting as if he was afraid Brad might change his mind.

"Go on back to the apartment," Brad said to the team. "Pete, go ahead and find out what you can about seaplane availability in the area. We'll have to make some allowance for picking up these things and loading them aboard, but I need to find out where we can pick them up first."

Willona hugged her husband fiercely and gave him a peck on the cheek.

"Go on back with the others, Ving. I'm going to stay with Brad and make sure he doesn't get taken by that slick salesman … and, besides, I have the checkbook. I want you to go back and work on some kind of plan that includes getting your hard-headed butt back here in one piece." She let him go and stalked toward the sales office.

Ving stared after her, shaking his head.

"Man, I hope that guy ate his Wheaties this morning. She is flat scary when she gets like that. He'll be lucky to get out of this with his commission."

Brad grinned and clapped his friend on the shoulder.

"Better him than us, brother. I'd rather take on the whole of JI with a P-38 and a plastic spoon than have her pissed at me."

* * *

The salesman assured him that there were several dealerships in Indonesia and that he could guarantee delivery within twenty-four hours to any one of several locations in Indonesia ... for a fee. Willona went to work on the poor man with a grin on her face that Brad was extremely happy was not directed at him. Ving was right; sweet, mild-natured Willona could be surprisingly scary.

* * *

On their return to Brad's apartment, Pete had gone straight to Brad's office to do some brief research on a model of seaplane that he thought might be capable of handling the mission. The closest thing he could find to what they needed was a Martin PBM-5 for sale or hire in Jakarta.

SEVEN

"The Polaris guy says he can get us two MRZR-D4s to a dealership in Makassar, South Sulawesi, Indonesia within twenty-four hours of the time we place the order and, of course, receives payment in full," Brad reported.

"Sneaky so-and-so tried to hold us up for more money to expedite the 'shipping', too, but I saw on his computer screen that the dealership in Makassar has several in stock already," Willona said with what might have been a sneer on her lovely face. She had set the salesman straight in record time and then negotiated the price down substantially. The sweating salesman had been relieved when they had left, even though Willona had not gone ahead with the purchase. "Let him sweat," she had responded to Brad's query about whether the deal would stand if they didn't go ahead with the purchase before returning to the apartment. "That turkey isn't going to get a dime until I know your travel arrangements. There's no sense committing until I'm sure that Grainger's check has cleared the account. I meant it when I said we aren't going out of pocket."

"Cleared the account?"

"Yes, unless he did a wire transfer, the monies will be marked 'pending' in your bank account. A check would remain pending until the transaction clears his bank and yours. I assume since they're in Midland that it would only take one night, but still…"

Brad held up his hands in surrender. He knew surprisingly little about the mechanisms of modern banking. "Got it, Willona. We don't spend any money until we confirm the retainer is in our account."

Willona smiled. "I'm glad we understand each other, Brad Jacobs! I'd hate to think I had to train you, this husband of mine was hard enough to educate." She gave Ving a loving glance before motioning for Pete to step away from Brad's desktop workstation. "I need to check the bank account Pete, go get yourself some coffee or something."

Vicky looked up from her laptop.

"We can catch a Delta Airlines flight to Makassar tonight if we leave by eight o'clock … there are three stops."

"Is one of them Jakarta?" Pete asked. "That's where the Mariner is and I haven't found anything else we can use closer than that."

Vicky's fingers pecked the keyboard of her laptop.

"Yes, that's the second stop," she said.

"The money's cleared, Brad," Willona said triumphantly. Brad's face changed almost magically. He was on firm ground again, completely in command of his team, confident, self-assured.

"Vicky, book us on the flight to Jakarta tonight. Pete, get with Willona after she finishes with the Polaris dealer and see what the guy wants for the PBM-5."

"You want to buy an airplane sight unseen, Brad?" Willona asked. "If we stretch, we might be able to afford it, but it would be smarter to go ahead and lease it instead." She turned to Pete. "That's a prop driven plane, right?" Pete nodded. "And can you fly it back here after the mission is over?" He shook his head no. She turned back to Brad. "You don't have to take my advice on this one, but it seems to me that if you wanted to buy an airplane you'd need something with enough range to make transatlantic flights and we can't swing that big a purchase just yet."

"No problem, Just lease it then." Brad, his decision made, turned his attention to Charlie. "You need to reach out to Daniel and see about setting up a meeting, small arms only. We need to do some more planning before we can give him a time and location, but he needs a heads up." Brad scratched his head. "Cash, tell him cash, U.S. dollars for the transaction." His preliminary instructions given, he motioned for the others to follow him out to the big table in the living room. They had an op order to formulate.

* * *

Brad got up from the table, stretching and yawning.

"I'm going to stretch my legs, guys. I'll be back in a few." He walked through the living room and out the sliding glass doors onto the patio. He shut the doors behind him. Charlie was busy sketching out a diagram of Camp Bashir as it had been when he had seen it three years before. He had protested that it had more than likely changed in the time since he had been there, but Brad had convinced him that any knowledge of the terrain and the camp was better than none at all and left him to his drawing.

He was trying to clear his mind so that he could approach the tactical phase of the op order planning fresh when he heard the door slide open and close behind him. He knew it was Willona even before she stepped in front of him.

"Before you get back in there and start your war planning, I needed to have a chat with you," she said.

Brad grinned at her.

"Talk away, Willona, you have my undivided attention."

"I'm serious, Brad. I want to know just how serious things are between you and Vicky."

"What brought that on?" he asked.

"Come on, Brad, I told you this was serious. I wouldn't be prying into your personal business if it wasn't and I think you know that."

Brad stared deep into her large, luminous brown eyes. He had known her almost as long as he'd known Ving, and she was closer to him than his own family had been, with the sole exception of his cousin Jessica.

"What do you want to know?" he asked finally.

"Is it permanent? Are you two planning on tying the knot?"

He thought his answer over very carefully before responding.

"I don't know for sure, Willona. We haven't discussed it really. If you're asking if I love her, I can only tell you that I've never felt this way about anybody else in my life. I think I'd like to spend the rest of my life with her, but I'm not sure, and I'm certainly not sure she feels that way about me." He paused. "Is it really important to you?"

"What makes it important is how it affects what I want to talk to you about."

"So go for it."

"I have a friend," she said slowly, choosing her words with great care. She loved Brad like a brother, but she felt as if she were walking through a minefield anyway. "He works in real estate and he says he has something special I should come see. I had a discussion with him last night over the phone and I gave him an idea of what I might—the operative word here being 'might'—be looking for. He sounded very excited, and when he described it, I got the idea that it would be perfect for you."

"So what's the problem?"

"Well, it's a distress sale of an estate, and the asking price is inconccivably low…"

"Sounds good to me, Willona, when are you going to go see it?"

"I didn't tell him, Brad, I said I needed to talk to you first."

"So go ahead, Willona, you didn't need to talk to me first. Hell, you've got my general power of attorney; you can do anything I could."

"That's just the thing, Brad, this place is unbelievably priced, but it's twenty acres near Dallas and the price, while really low for the property, is higher than we can afford to pay cash for. There is a way we could swing it anyway though…"

Brad beamed at her.

"Out with it, woman!"

"Brad, if we sold your apartment and your warehouse, we could probably swing the balance out of our reserves with no problem."

"Where would I live?"

"That's not a problem. Stanley says the property is just what I described. There's a five-bedroom house with a mother-in-law plan, a huge six-car garage, a sixteen-thousand-square-foot barn, and assorted outbuildings, all in excellent shape."

Brad looked thoughtful.

"I think, from what I heard, Brad, that we could convert part of the barn to a real office and still leave you a warehouse that is ten times larger than the one you have now," she said excitedly. Her enthusiasm was catching.

Brad shrugged.

"If it's as you've described it, it's okay with me, Willona."

She hugged him, squeezing him tightly.

"You won't regret this, Brad. I haven't seen it yet, but Stanley is taking pictures today and he's going to email them to me when he gets home. If it looks the way he's described it, I'll take a ride out there tomorrow and do a walk through."

"Just how far outside Dallas is this place?"

"It's up just south of Corral City, just above Grapevine Lake, about thirty miles out."

He was familiar with the area, and he liked it. He cocked his head to one side, as if he was mulling it over, but he'd already decided. Finally, he decided it wasn't fair to leave her hanging any longer; she was obviously excited at the prospect. He wondered if there was something she wasn't telling him, but he trusted her.

"Do whatever you think is right, Willona," he said, smiling at her. "I trust your judgment."

He didn't mention the conversation to any of the others when he went back inside, he wanted them focused on the mission.

* * *

James Ardmore, C.I.A. Deputy Director of Operations for Southeast Asia, nervously walked down the corridor in C.I.A. Headquarters, Langley, Virginia towards the office of the director. He was nervous because in the five years he had occupied his position the director had never summoned him before. Usually the director only communicated with him by memo or, if he was feeling particularly chummy, over a secure landline. The director rarely felt chummy. Ardmore felt in his suit jacket pocket for the package of antacid tablets he kept there for crises. There was a box of similar packages in his top left-hand drawer back in his own rather opulent office … there was always an overabundance of crises at the C.I.A.

As he hesitantly fingered the little tube of antacids, he wondered exactly what kind of crisis had compelled the director to summon him personally. It was not a comforting thought, it couldn't be anything good. Ardmore snatched the paper tube out of his pocket and thumbed several of the minty smelling tablets into his palm then popped them into his mouth. He chewed furiously for a few seconds and then popped two more into his mouth.

The director's secretary's secretary was seated in the outer office, and she directed Ardmore to a chair while she telephoned the director's secretary. She spoke into the phone for a few seconds and then hung up. Ignoring Ardmore, she fiddled with several manila folders on her desk and answered her phone a couple of times (speaking imperiously into the handset each time) until an intercom buzzer sounded. She punched a button to shut off the buzzer and motioned haughtily for Ardmore to pass through the highly polished oak double doors behind her. She glanced back down and didn't even speak as he went to the doors and twisted one of the huge brass doorknobs.

The director's secretary's office was even larger than his own, her desk larger, her furnishings more sumptuous, and he recognized the artwork on the dark paneled walls as originals. There was a large oil painting of the director on one of the walls, right next to the obligatory poster-sized photos of the president and the rest of the chain of command. The secretary didn't even glance up at him, just motioned with her hand for him to take a seat. The leather wingback chair was stiff and uncomfortable. Ardmore saw from the ubiquitous government-issue clock on the wall that it was three p.m.

At precisely three thirty-seven the intercom on the secretary's desk buzzed, and she pressed a button beside it. Ardmore heard a loud clicking sound from the doors behind her, and she indicated he should go inside with a curt nod of her head. She never even looked up.

The director's office was huge, and his desktop was formed of a polished slab of black granite supported by a mahogany frame.

"James, so good to see you," the director said, actually getting up from his custom built red leather orthopedic chair and stepping out from behind his desk, a false, glad-handing politician's smile on his face. "It's been a long time." Ardmore had never been closer to the director than the length of the conference room down the hall. "Have a seat, James; we have a little problem to discuss."

Ardmore's stomach roiled with acid as he sat in another royally uncomfortable leather wingback chair, this one a good foot shorter than the one the director sat in. He wished he had eaten a few more of the antacid tablets.

The director sat down and clasped his hands in front of him, intertwining all his fingers except for his two forefingers, which he placed together pointing upwards like a church steeple.

"James, do you remember Stanley Povitch … from your section? He retired a year or so ago."

Ardmore did, just barely, recollect a balding, pudgy little man who rarely spoke to anyone at the agency. Rumor had it that he was a snitch for the director, and, as a consequence, his coworkers had avoided him like the plague. Ardmore, who left his office about as frequently as the director left his, had never had any direct contact with the man and had never wanted to.

"Yes sir." There was no other answer he could give, lest the director get the impression that he wasn't on the ball.

"It seems that Stanley has taken a position with Duckworth International Petroleum down in Midland, Texas. Are you familiar with them?"

"Of course sir," Ardmore answered, his unease growing by the second. There had been a minor note on the daily summary put together by his staff that morning, but for the life of him he couldn't remember what it referred to.

"Good, good. Listen, James, we have an operation going on in Kalimantan somewhere. It's being run through our cultural attaché in Brunei, and it's classified Top Secret: VP. The VP stands for vice presidential, this op is his and you are not at liberty to even acknowledge the classification."

Indignance rose in Ardmore's stomach along with acid and bile.

"There's a highly classified op going on in my zone and I have not even been apprised of it?"

The director nodded.

"That's right, James, and you're not being apprised of it now. This op is running at the direction of the vice president, and the details are being released on a 'need to know' basis only. All you need to know is that there is a private security company in Dallas that is about to stick its nose into something it would be better that they not become involved in. Stanley is still loyal to me, and this afternoon he informed me that our counterpart in Indonesia has a loose cannon in their midst who has been in contact with a member of this security company and is about to help them throw a monkey wrench into our op.

"What I need for you to do," he said, sliding a sealed manila envelope across his desk to Ardmore, "is to pass this information on to our cultural attaché in Brunei and have him take care of the situation … personally. Now listen to me very carefully: use a courier. There is an F-22 standing by at Andrews

Air Force Base for the first leg of his journey, which is to be effected as quickly as humanly possible. It is absolutely imperative that the courier not be made aware of the contents of this envelope *nor of its origination.* Is that clear, James?"

Ardmore swallowed, with difficulty, before he answered. This was a nightmare scenario, right out of a badly written spy movie. Frankly, it smelled. He managed to keep a straight face, despite the fact that he was scared shitless. The only thing that would show if someone eventually tried to backtrace this envelope would be the signature of the dispatching authority who had ordered the courier to deliver it—one James Arthur Ardmore Jr.

EIGHT

The flight would last for over twenty-eight hours, including a brief layover in L.A. and a six-hour layover in Tokyo, but the first stop would be in Los Angeles at LAX, two hours and forty-five minutes after they took off from Dallas.

"I hate flying this time of night," Vicky whispered. She was sitting next to Brad in first class, sipping champagne and holding tightly to his free hand.

"It wouldn't be so bad if the first leg wasn't so short," Brad murmured, sipping at his own champagne. Vicky had scheduled them all first class for the entire trip. The team understood that they were free to drink, sparingly, on the first two legs of the flight. The booze would no longer be acceptable after their arrival at Haneda International Airport in Tokyo. They were professionals.

At LAX, they switched over to a massive new Boeing 767–200 bound for Tokyo. Vicky promptly ordered another glass of champagne as well as a blanket and a pillow. Before they were an hour into the second leg, she was fast asleep. For the next eleven hours Brad, unable to make himself sleep, focused his considerable intellect on Willona's plans for Jacobs & Ving Security LLC first and then on the mission itself. He was committed to the mission, and he believed that the plan the team had come up with had a better-than-average chance of working … but something he couldn't quite pinpoint kept nagging at the back of his mind. There was a piece of the puzzle missing, but he was damned if he could figure out what it was.

* * *

The soft sound of a bell and the captain's voice coming over the speakers woke Brad up, and the quiet hum of the engines backed off a notch as the aircraft began its descent to Tokyo Haneda

International Airport. He reached across Vicky's still sleeping body and raised the shutter. Brilliant sunshine washed over his face and it took a moment for his eyes to focus. A breathtaking view of the majestic Mount Fuji greeted him, and he gently shook Vicky awake so that she could share it with him.

The captain repeated his instructions in Japanese as the team awakened and scrabbled to fold up blankets and pass pillows to the flight attendants, who were scurrying up and down the aisles collecting the odds and ends left over from the long overseas flight.

The ultramodern international flight terminal at Haneda was awe-inspiring, but they took no time to gawk at the sights. They had a six-hour layover at Haneda, so Vicky had booked three transit double rooms at the Royal Park Transit Hotel so that the team could shower, change, and stretch before catching the flight to Soekarno-Hatta

International Airport in Jakarta. Ving, Jared, and Pete went into one of the rooms, Charlie and Jessica took the second, and Vicky and Brad occupied the third.

"I think we should take advantage of this opportunity, Brad, don't you?" Vicky asked as soon as the door closed behind them. She kicked off her shoes and started walking towards the bathroom, dropping clothes suggestively as she sashayed across the room. Brad watched in aroused fascination as the last vestige of her clothing, a wispy piece of lace that showed off more than it concealed, dropped around her ankles and she daintily stepped out of them. "Are you coming?" she asked breezily.

"Not yet," Brad growled deep in his throat as he tore off his dark polo shirt and kicked off his shoes.

* * *

Track Down Borneo

The flight to Soekarno-Hatta was uneventful but pleasant, the team well rested. Only Charlie had seen the area before, so whenever the aircraft was not over water, all eyes were glued to the windows. Every square inch of land beneath them was lush, green, and beautiful.

As soon as they came off the jetway in Jakarta they were met by a short, potbellied man wearing a sleeveless grey T-shirt and a battered and grimy captain's hat with tarnished gold braid on its visor perched at a cocky angle on top of his head. An unlit, half-smoked cigar was clenched between his teeth. Both Vicky and Jessica kept as far away from the man as possible, all the while giving him dubious looks. Pete, however, greeted the grubby man like a long-lost buddy, giving him a hearty clap on the shoulder and then a bear hug.

"We've never met, Brad," Pete said by way of introduction, "but Herb here is Tiny Wilcox's brother ... you remember Tiny, don't you?" Tiny

Wilcox was anything but, and Brad remembered the Marine corporal very well. Tiny had been one of the finest E.O.D. (Explosive Ordnance Disposal) men Brad had ever had the pleasure of working with. Tiny had met an untimely death during the second battle of Fallujah when a radio detonated I.E.D. (Improvised Explosive Device) had been set off virtually beneath his feet in an alleyway.

Herb, it turned out, had been the beneficiary of Tiny's Servicemembers's Group Life Insurance (SGLI) policy. Herb Wilcox had been an enlisted man in the Army, serving in South Korea at the time of his brother's death, and when he had separated, he had moved to Jakarta instead of going back to the U.S. After a short time, he'd decided to stay in Jakarta and had purchased the Martin PBM-5 with the check and started his own charter business.

"I rarely take charters myself anymore," Herb explained as he led them out to the parking lot where a battered carryall was parked. "Business is booming and I've got three newer birds in the air right this minute." Jessica gave the pudgy man a skeptical glance and then turned to Vicky in the third seat and mouthed the word "windbag" silently. Vicky didn't respond.

Herb drove fast, but not excessively so, and soon the carryall was turning into a driveway leading to a very large, well-maintained Quonset on a fairly isolated beach. There was a large tarmac pad in front of the Quonset hut, and a small army of construction workers were building a second, much longer airstrip beside the original tarmac strip. The original strip ran down to a dock jutting out into the water. A Martin PBM-5 in absolutely pristine condition, in stark contrast to Herb, was parked on the apron in front of the Quonset hut.

"She's in great shape," Herb boasted, waving one fat hand in the general direction of the PBM-5. "I do all the maintenance work on Louise personally.

The airframe has been modified to accommodate the larger door under the wing, just as you specified."

"Louise?" Ving asked.

"My mother's name," Herb said, frowning slightly. "She passed when Tiny and I were kids. I named my first plane after her hoping it would bring me luck—" his face cleared and he chewed on the still unlit cigar stub as he smiled around it "—and it has!"

"If she's such a great bird and has so much sentimental value to you, why are you selling her?" Brad asked as he, Pete, and Ving walked up to study the sturdy old aircraft.

Herb grinned.

"I got a line on a sweet Gulfstream business jet with only a hundred hours on it since it was completely overhauled, that's why I got a construction crew extending my runway. I need the cash from the sale of this baby to make up the rest of the down payment on the jet 'cause construction labor ain't cheap, even here in Jakarta."

Pete grunted.

"Business must really be good."

Herb's grin got wider.

"Yep."

"Looks good to me, Brad, I say we go for it," Pete remarked.

Brad turned to Herb.

"How long before we can go wheels up?"

"About twenty minutes after you sign the paperwork."

"Let's do it."

The charter agreement signed and the credit card transaction completed, Brad and Pete followed Herb on a walk around the PBM-5 while he completed his preflight inspection. The rest of the team stretched and did calisthenics to try to overcome the effects of the long flight. When the preflight was completed, Pete and Herb boarded the aircraft and ran up the engines while Brad walked over to collect the rest of the team.

"Are you sure that thing can even fly?" Jessica asked dubiously. "It looks old."

"It is," Brad chuckled, "but Pete did his homework. Herb has a great reputation as a pilot and a mechanic, and his safety record is impeccable. That bird has been carefully rebuilt from the ground up, has modern avionics, and Herb has installed updates that weren't available at the time those planes were in use. There aren't many of them left flying, but Pete has assured me there's not another one like this in existence." He added, "Pete says it's okay and I trust him."

"Pete's going to fly it?" Vicky seemed a little dubious too.

"Pete's going to be the copilot, Vicky, and Pete can fly anything that will move through the air."

"If you say so…"

Jared spoke up.

"If Pete says it's okay, it's okay. I'm gonna grab my stuff and find me a comfortable place to stretch out in that big ol' critter. She ain't gonna be as sweet a ride as them jets we got here on." He turned and walked back to the carryall to get his rucksack.

"We ain't gonna get nothin' done standin' around here jawin'," Ving muttered. Then he turned to follow Jared to the carryall. Brad, Vicky, and Jessica trailed after them.

*   *   *

Herb made a final trip to his office in the Quonset hut and came back out to the aircraft holding four military topographical maps of Kalimantan and handed them to Brad, apologizing for not being able to acquire more. Brad was grateful for them, realizing that he had not considered bringing along a backup for the GPS systems in his phones. He cursed himself inwardly for not taking that detail into consideration and wondered what else he might have forgotten.

*   *   *

The huge Pratt & Whitney R-2800 Double Wasp twin-row, 18-cylinder, air-cooled radial aircraft engines roared as Pete advanced the throttles. Herb let off the brakes as Pete lowered the flaps and the massive flying boat began to rumble down the runway towards the Java Sea.

Jessica was uneasy when she felt the big craft begin to rock in the water, and she was really uncomfortable when the engines roared even louder and the plane began to move across the water. The sound of the waves slamming against the metal of the hull terrified her, and her stomach lurched when the big bird hopped once, twice, three times before it leaped into the air. For a moment she struggled to control the churning in her stomach, but it was too little too late. Vicky salvaged some of her dignity by holding a seasick bag in front of her mouth as she hurled. Charles held her shoulders.

"Didn't expect that," Jared drawled.

"Nope," Ving remarked. "She didn't get that discombobulated even when she was shot, down in the Amazon." He reached into his rucksack and withdrew a plastic-wrapped package, which he passed to Jared. "Bacon sammich?"

"Sure," Jared said, reaching for the sandwich and unwrapping it before putting it to his mouth and taking a big bite.

Vicky stared at the duo in disbelief for a moment, and then she, too, had to scramble for another barf bag.

"Well, I'll be damned," Ving remarked, chewing on a mouthful of bacon and bread.

* * *

Brad sat in the jump seat behind the pilot's and copilot's seats, watching the numerous dials, lights, and gauges as Herb leveled the aircraft off and Pete retarded the throttles just a hair. The engines seemed to smooth out and Pete and Herb fiddled with switches and toggles until the bird was trimmed up and flying smoothly. All the lights were in the green, which Brad knew meant that everything was running right. Despite his faith in Pete, Brad heaved a sigh of relief. He was acutely aware that he was flying at thirteen thousand feet in the air at something approaching two hundred miles per hour in an aircraft built for the government by the lowest bidder some fifty-odd years before. The thought was not a comforting one.

Another uncomfortable thought crashed into the forefront of his mind, and despite his intention to keep his reservations to himself, he had to ask a question.

"Didn't these things require a third flight crew member?" he yelled above the roar of the engine. It had occurred to him that the jump seat his ass was resting on had been installed for a reason—a place for a flight engineer or a navigator to sit.

"Yeah," Herb yelled back then pointed at a set of headphones hanging from a rack, indicating that Brad should put them on. Brad did as he was told.

"There, that better?" Herb asked.

The engine noise had diminished to a dull rumble and there was not the slightest hint of static in the headset.

"Wow, yeah! Much better."

"Good. In answer to your question, yes, the specs called for a flight crew of three, but with the upgrades and modifications I've made, we only need two."

"She's a sweet ride all right," Pete chimed in. "Maybe we should talk to Willona about buying this thing after all, Brad."

"Bad as I need to sell her, Pete, I don't think that's such a good idea. To get her back to the States you'd have to take her apart and ship her back to Texas. I don't even want to try to think about what that would cost, and I don't know another person in the world I would trust to put her back together again." He patted the console as if the aircraft was a living thing. "She's a good old girl, and I trust her with my life, but I don't think she could stand that kind of trauma at her age."

Partially comforted, Brad settled back for the four-hour flight to Makassar.

NINE

The rest of the flight was smooth as glass, without even any turbulence to disturb them. Their descent was smooth and controlled, with Pete grinning at the wheel as Herb let him bring it down. His smile faded when Herb announced he was taking control, but Pete was a wise and experienced aviator, so he raised both hands off the wheel to show he had relinquished control of the craft.

Brad watched anxiously out the windscreen as the white-capped water of the Makassar Strait rushed up at them. The plane jerked violently as the hull struck the surface and bounced, hard, once, twice, three times before it stayed down. Hank idled towards a stretch of bare sandy beach, and Brad wondered briefly how the hell they were going to get into the town. He didn't have to wonder long.

Herb and Pete shut down the engines and Brad walked back into the cargo area to check on the rest of the team. He found Ving and Jared fast asleep on the aluminum floor of the fuselage. Vicky and Charlie were holding a green-faced Jessica between them, and there were a couple of full airsick bags on the floor near them.

Vicky looked up at him.

"We'd better get some Dramamine pills while we're on the ground, Brad. This may be a wonderful old aircraft, but Jessica's tummy doesn't like it." Brad carefully hid his smile. He had never admitted to anyone that he became violently ill before every HALO jump, though he was pretty sure Ving knew. He sympathized with Jessica, but he would never let her know it, nor would he give her a hard time about it.

Minutes later, an ancient Checker Marathon rolled onto the beach beside the PBM-5 and a smiling man waved at Herb.

"I'll stay here with Louise, Pete. Hasan will take you to the Polaris dealership. Don't pay him, no matter what he tells you, I've already taken care of him. You can trust him to take you to the dealership, but don't let him con you into letting him take you somewhere else. Got it?"

*   *   *

The sign on the outside of the dealership declared in Indonesian, Javanese, and English that it would be three hours before they opened their doors.

"Damn it! How could I have missed that?" Brad fumed.

"Sorry Brad, I should have remembered. They eat dinner late in Indonesia, and they get up later too." Charlie glanced down at his watch. "We're lucky they open as early as they do."

"Three hours!" Ving grumbled. "A man can't be expected to sit around half the day with no groceries…"

"Come off it, Ving," Vicky groused. "I saw you eating your bacon sandwiches on the plane!"

"Me too!" Jessica groaned miserably.

"But … that was, well, that was hours ago!" Ving seemed to be genuinely anguished.

"I doubt there're any restaurants open this early around here, Ving," said Charlie, "but I saw some street vendors a few blocks back."

"I don't care; I could eat a damned horse."

"You're not going to find any bacon here, Ving," Charlie cautioned, "at least not from a street vendor. I've heard you can get it in a very few places now, but we're not near any of them and they wouldn't be open anyway. You need to remember a couple of things when you buy from a street vendor though…"

"I'm all ears, Charlie."

"First, prepare yourself for the fact that just about everything you can get for breakfast is going to have rice in it."

"I can live with rice, I like rice."

"Second, if it smells good, eat it … but don't ask what's in it."

"Don't know if I like that or not."

"Just take my word for it, Ving. If you want to keep it down, don't ask what's in it."

"Damn, I was just beginning to get my appetite back," Vicky moaned. Jared roared with laughter.

* * *

Charlie was right. They found a row of street vendors not far from the dealership, and virtually everything was made of rice or contained it. Charlie bought his breakfast first, something that had wooden skewers of what looked and smelled and tasted like fried chicken on a bed of white rice. Jessica sniffed at it but made a face and refused to taste it.

"Try the congee," Charlie muttered through a mouthful of food. "You need to eat because you lost everything in your stomach already, but you need to remember we'll be getting back on Louise for the last leg in a couple of hours. Maybe, with the Dramamine, that rice gruel will stay down."

Jessica sniffed at the stuff, and the vendor, sensing a possible sale, put a tiny portion on a thin sheet of rice flour dough and offered it for her to taste. Jessica liked it and held up a single finger, indicating she wanted one portion. Only Charlie seemed to notice the vendor holding back a part of the order almost exactly the same size as the 'free' sample. He said nothing, happy that Jessica was eating at all.

Ving leaned over the cart of the vendor who had sold Charlie the skewered meat and inhaled deeply. The aroma made his mouth water.

"What—"

"Don't ask, Ving," Charlie warned. "Just order some if you like the smell. I promise, whatever it is, it tastes great." He had absolutely no intention of telling the big man that the meat was indeed chicken, and he wondered if he'd have the balls to tease Ving later by telling him it was rat meat.

* * *

Once back at the dealership they were greeted effusively by the manager who was always happy to make a sale, even if it was one he'd been forced to share the profit on.

"Are they ready?"

"They are, most assuredly, sir." The manager was practically fawning over him. "Please sir, come this way." Brad followed the man out of the showroom and into a shop filled with frenetic activity. Just inside the rear door were two brand new MRZR-D4s, still inside their shipping crates.

"I was told these would be ready to go," Brad said unpleasantly.

"It will be only a matter of minutes, sir," the manager said apologetically. He turned and spoke harshly in Javanese to a pair of mechanics, who instantly leaped towards the crates and began ripping them open.

Charlie didn't speak more than a few words of Javanese, but he recognized the word "barbarian" when he heard it. He motioned Pete over and whispered in his ear.

"Watch them closely. I don't know what he told those guys, but I know he doesn't much like us."

Pete grunted his acknowledgement and squatted down to stare at the two men as they worked. Charlie moved over to stand beside Brad and whisper what he'd heard.

The mechanics, under the watchful eyes of the team, stripped away the cardboard and then the wooden outer frame until Pete stopped them. "Tell them to leave 'em on the pallets," he ordered the manager.

"But sir, he said—" The manager was pointing at Brad.

"Leave them on the pallets, like he said," Brad ordered, though he looked questioningly at Pete.

"Have you got anyone in this shop who can weld aluminum?" Pete asked.

The manager looked surprised then jabbered at one of the mechanics, who bowed and raced across the shop, coming back with an older man in khaki pants and a strappy T-shirt.

Pete glanced around the shop until he located a flat piece of cardboard and a black magic marker. Quickly, he sketched out a drawing of two oblongs with metal tongues protruding from one end. "Can you make these?" he asked, tapping the drawings. The old man cocked his head to one side, studying the drawings. "Aluminum," Pete said, tapping the drawings. "Can … you … make … these … for … me … out … of … aluminum?" He said each word slowly and clearly, tapping the drawings at each word.

The old man rocked back on his heels and cupped his chin as if he was thinking.

"Quarter inch or three eighths?" he asked in perfect English. "They're ramps, right? How long do you need them?"

Pete was both stunned and embarrassed, but Brad and the others were laughing uproariously. The old man allowed himself the briefest of sly smiles and then motioned Pete over to a worktable, where he pulled out a drafting pad and instruments. The two men bent over the drafting table and put their heads together, talking animatedly.

"If you will come with me," the manager said politely, "we will see about getting you all some coffee while we wait. Also, we will need to discuss prices, as these ramps were not part of our deal." He turned and walked away without looking back. He had the walk of a salesman who knew he had lost and then regained the upper hand. Brad knew he was about to get clobbered on the price for fabricating the ramps, which Pete had never mentioned, but he was pleased that they were still on schedule.

Before they concluded their business, the manager had sent his assistant out to purchase some Dramamine for Jessica, for which, of course, he added a small fee to Brad's bill.

* * *

The manager was more than willing to provide them with a ride back to Louise on the delivery truck, for which he added only a nominal fee, probably no more than twice what it would have cost them to take a taxi. The reason for Pete wanting the Mrazors left on their pallets became obvious when a forklift placed both of them on the bed of the truck. Brad and the others watched in fascination as the forklift driver then drove around to the back of the truck and inserted the lifting arms into steel pockets beneath the bed, and then lifted itself up off the ground. The driver attached chains from the forklift to the back of the truck and then waved for the team to get aboard before he climbed into the cab of the truck.

Brad had been a little concerned that the Mrazors would be too large and too heavy for them to load them aboard the aircraft, but the forklift made quick work of the task. The pallets slipped through the door with inches to spare, and they were able to shove the first one forward across the aluminum deck with little effort. Once the pallets were loaded, Herb and Pete secured them to the deck with three-inch-wide nylon cargo straps.

Brad had not seen Pete take any measurements for the ramps, but apparently the man had calibrating eyes. The simple ramps were designed to be slid into the fuselage and then secured to the floor for storage in flight. Pete and the driver unloaded the ramps and fitted them to the bottom of the doorway. They fit perfectly.

"Once we land, the ramps can be slid into place and we can drive the Mrazors down onto the sand or even into the water if necessary," Pete explained proudly.

TEN

The last leg of the flight, from Makassar to Sebamban, would take roughly an hour depending on whether they had a headwind or a tailwind. Herb had arranged for a fuel truck to fill up his tanks on the beach in Makassar because he knew the large aircraft would consume a great deal of fuel flying at wave top level to stay under the radar.

Ving slept while Jared busied himself honing his already razor-sharp combat knife. Jessica sat on the deck with her legs crossed and her head down. She was beginning to regret eating the street vendor's congee, but the Dramamine enabled her to keep it down despite her stomach's active rebellion. There was a lot of turbulence at sea level. Brad, Charlie, and Vicky huddled together on the deck of the cargo compartment and discussed the upcoming scheduled meeting with Charlie's contact.

"I hope your trust in this guy is not misplaced," Brad said. "But I'm not as worried about that as I am about the *Kesatuan Penjagaan Laut dan Pantai.*" (Indonesian Sea and Coast Guard, KPLP.)

Charlie grunted.

"We won't have to worry much about the KPLP, they mostly deal with shipping and navigation matters. The guys we have to worry about are in the Maritime Security Agency, BAKAMLA." (*Badan Keamanan Laut Republik.*) He thought for a moment. "I really don't expect to see them either. That's a huge stretch of coastline, and there aren't many roads into the interior there. That's why JI located their training base in the area. For the most part, smugglers and pirates control that part of the island's coast, and they usually operate up north, towards Balikpapan. BAKAMLA is really pathetically underfunded."

Privately, Brad was concerned because they were entering the country unarmed, but he was more concerned about having no option other than dealing with a black market arms dealer with whom he was unfamiliar. He was placing a lot of faith in Charlie's contact … and in Charlie's judgment.

* * *

The water was shallow and very choppy when Herb set Louise down on the water; the big bird shuddered and hopped when it touched down. The racket was terrifying and they were all grateful when the ordeal was finally over. Herb guided the aircraft over to a narrow beach of hard packed sand and trundled it up out of the water and onto the beach.

Brad and Jared opened the door and jumped onto the beach before Herb even brought Louise to a complete stop, while the others set to releasing the cargo straps from the Mrazors and readying them for offloading.

Brad moved to the left of the aircraft, while Jared moved to the right, and both moved quickly into the wood line. Brad had read that Borneo was one of the most biodiverse environments in the world, but, even so, he was completely unprepared for the spectacle that greeted him. The palm trees at the edge of the beach were no surprise. The mix of deciduous and evergreen trees just inside the line of palms was a surprise, some of them as tall as the skyscrapers back home in Dallas.

The seemingly deserted area was literally crawling with animal and bird life. Before he lost sight of the sandy beach he had spotted monkeys, an orangutan, parrots, a wild pig, and various other small animals he couldn't identify. None of them showed any fear of the two-legged human invading their home, and many of them eyed him curiously.

The flowers were incredible, a riotous explosion of beauty and color. There were startling varieties of orchids and carnivorous pitcher plants, as well as more ominous looking species with sharp thorns and possibly poisonous oils greasing their stems and leaves. It was as if he had stepped into the most concentrated natural history museum on Earth.

Forcing himself to focus on the task at hand, Brad turned left and made his way about two hundred yards through the forest, parallel to the beach, before turning left again to make his way back to the beach. He saw more varieties of animal and bird, but no sign that man had ever trod there. It was a humbling experience that made him wonder if that had been the way the world looked when Adam and Eve were created. He was deeply affected by the foray, feeling a kind of reverence for the unspoiled beauty.

A flock of seagulls, soaring and wheeling over the sand, greeted him when he walked between the palms back onto the beach. The sound of the aircraft engines, somewhat muted inside the tree line, intruded on his reverie and brought him back to his mission mindset. Far down the beach, past the PBM-5's fuselage, he could see Jared hurrying back toward the aircraft. Brad picked up his pace.

The first of the aluminum ramps slid slowly out of the open door and touched down on the sand as he marched toward the plane. He thought the angle of the ramp was a little steep, telling him that Pete should have made them a foot or two longer. Crossing his fingers, he hoped the precarious angle wouldn't prove a problem. The second ramp slid out as he and Jared met beneath the wing of the bird.

"Looks kinda steep," Jared shouted over the roar of Louise's engines.

"Yeah. Hope that doesn't cause a problem," Brad shouted back.

Jared leaped aboard the aircraft and a moment later Brad saw the front wheels of the first Mrazor creep slowly out onto the ramps. He heard Pete yell and then saw the big pilot's hand slip out from beneath the Mrazor holding the metal hook end of one of the yellow nylon cargo straps and attach it to the first crossmember of the left ramp. A moment later, Pete repeated the performance by running another yellow cargo strap beneath the right front of the Mrazor and attaching it to the first crossmember of the right ramp.

Slowly, the Mrazor inched its way out onto the ramps, and Brad held his breath as Jared jockeyed the 1900-pound vehicle to the sand, the stout three-eighths-inch aluminum side rails of the ramps bending slightly beneath the weight. He started breathing again when the back wheels of the Mrazor rolled onto the sand. Jared goosed the throttle exuberantly and the powerful vehicle kicked up a small roostertail of sand as he cleared the way for the second Mrazor.

The second Mrazor proved to be a bit more difficult from the very beginning. First, the team had trouble disengaging the ratchet strap that secured the pallet to the rings on the deck in the aircraft. Once they got the ratchet to release, it proved nearly impossible to swivel the pallet around so that the nose of the Mrazor faced the open door. Finally, Pete sat down with his back braced against the fuselage and used his legs to get the pallet moving. Once the pallet began to move, the rest of the team swiveled it around, bringing it to rest on the lip of the doorframe.

Ving climbed into the driver's seat and cranked the Mrazor's turbo diesel engine and then promptly stalled it out. It took a while for the diesel fuel to clear before he could start it again, and when he did, Brad could hear the catcalls from the team over the roar of the idling engines

Ving managed to get both front wheels started on the ramps with no problem, but as the back wheels rolled clear of the doorframe the left ramp began to sink into the sand under the weight of the heavy Mrazor.

"Look out, Ving!" Brad screamed.

Ving started in surprise and jerked the steering wheel inadvertently. The Mrazor started an inexorable slide to the left, and before Ving realized what was happening, the machine tilted and suddenly hurtled down onto the sand and toppled over onto its side with Ving still behind the steering wheel.

"Shit!" Jared yelled as he raced toward Ving. Brad was right behind him.

Unhurt but royally pissed off, Ving managed to stagger to his feet, furious and cursing.

"Are you all right?" Brad called out.

"Son of a *bitch!*" Ving swore, holding his left shoulder, stomping around in circles while Brad and Jared chased after him brushing at the sand that coated Ving's pants and shirt. One after another the rest of the team leaped out the door of the aircraft and hurried over to see if Ving was okay. When it was determined that he was uninjured, Pete walked over to the Mrazor to see what, if any, damage had been done to it.

"Get Herb out of here, Pete, we'll check the Mrazor out," Brad yelled. Pete nodded and trotted up to the door and leaped in. He trotted forward to the cockpit and tapped Herb on the shoulder then gave him a thumbs up. Five minutes later, Herb had Louise skimming across the chop and headed toward the Siring Park Sea off Taman Siring Laut, 50 odd miles north-northeast of the spot where he had left Team Dallas. There he would wait for the Team's call for extraction.

Vicky started it. Once she was assured that Ving wasn't hurt, she began to smile at his continued agitation. Jessica was the next to smile, and then, unable to help themselves, Jared and Pete started to laugh. Ving glared at them and continued to swear colorfully. When Brad, tongue in cheek, remarked that Willona was going to pitch a fit if Ving had damaged the Mrazor, the team collapsed in raucous laughter at the stung look Ving gave him. After a few more moments of fuming, Ving's good nature asserted itself and he began to see the humor in the situation. It wasn't long before he collapsed on the beach, laughing hysterically along with the others.

The team quickly loaded up the two Mrazors, cranked up the quiet turbo diesel motors, and disappeared into the forest, making for the outskirts of Sebamban where Charlie had arranged to meet his contact.

* * *

The Mrazors were concealed behind a mud and wattle outbuilding and the team was spread out in a thicket of ferns and scattered palms. Brad and

Charlie were closest to the meeting point, lying prone behind a fallen palm log. Brad held a pair of compact Zeiss binoculars to his eyes. A plume of dust rose over the road approaching the deserted farmstead.

"Not very inconspicuous," Brad muttered as a shiny black civilian version of a Humvee rolled into the yard in front of the empty, burned-out house.

"Daniel's cover lets him get away with a lot," Charlie said, standing up as soon as Daniel opened the door of the Humvee and stepped out of it. At the same time, the passenger side door opened and another man, dark-complexioned and dressed like a character out of the 1990s show *Miami Vice*, stepped out of the vehicle. "Must be our gunrunner," Charlie remarked, waving at his friend.

Brad had put away his binoculars and had begun to rise from his prone position when a back door on the passenger side of the Hummer opened and a man in a tailored blue suit, white shirt, black tie, and aviator sunglasses stepped out, carrying a slim leather briefcase.

"Jesus!" Brad exclaimed, "Get down, Charlie!" It was a helpless feeling, not having a weapon other than the combat knife he carried in his boot, but he drew it anyway.

Daniel froze when he saw Charlie drop to the ground.

"It's okay, Charlie, he just wants to talk to Brad!" Daniel said, a sheepish look on his face. The gunrunner looked just as aggravated as Brad felt.

Blue suit stepped forward, holding up a diplomatic carnet opened to expose an official identification card.

"Brad Jacobs?" he called out. "Lawrence P. Waldingham III. I'm the cultural attaché at the U.S. Embassy in Brunei." He continued walking towards Brad and Charlie, careful to keep both his hands in plain sight.

"Cultural attaché my ass," Brad muttered. He knew that the C.I.A. loved planting their personnel in embassies throughout the world as 'cultural attachés'. There was no love lost between Brad Jacobs and the C.I.A. He had to consider that the mission had been compromised.

ELEVEN

Daniel Novianti closed the distance between himself and Charlie, coming to a halt in front of his friend with his head down.

"I brought Lorenzo as promised, my friend, but the asshat from your embassy was forced on me by my own superiors," he said in a low voice that did not carry very far. "You have to believe me, I had no choice." His face bore a very sincere pained look.

"Which one of you is Brad Jacobs?" the 'cultural attaché' demanded rudely.

"That would be me," Brad drawled. He'd placed his hands in his trousers pockets, mostly to hide the fact that his fists were clenched and his knuckles were white. His eyes were narrow and cold and the whole team could see that he was barely managing to contain his fury.

The attaché gestured imperiously for Brad to come forward, and everyone held their breath, wondering if Brad would explode. Instead, he turned away from the attaché, walked about thirty feet away from the team, and turned to give the attaché a supremely insolent look that said, "If you want to talk to me, come over here." He said nothing.

Furious and humiliated, the attaché held his ground until he could see that Brad would not come to him; then he stalked over to where Brad stood and hissed at him.

"I'm here to inform you that you are about to compromise an operation that has been a long time in planning and execution, a mission directed by the highest offices in the United States government."

"Just who the hell are you?" Brad asked.

Track Down Borneo

"Lawrence P. Waldingham III. I'm the cultural attaché at the U.S. Embassy in Brunei. I already told you that!" Waldingham said indignantly.

"Mr. Waldingham, I'm a private citizen of the United States going about my personal business, and unless you can give me a more compelling reason than that I'm 'compromising' some super-secret operation ordered by some high muckety-muck in Washington that you have yet to identify, I'm about to invite you to kiss my ass."

Waldingham drew himself up to his full five feet ten inches and positively bristled with self-importance.

"Mr. Jacobs, I am *ordering* you to cease and desist this minute. I am not at liberty to disclose either the nature of the operation, the level of classification or who originated it!"

Brad turned and pointed at Ving then waved for him to come over. Ving walked up beside the attaché and stopped next to him. The attaché looked distinctly uneasy.

"Mr. Waldingham, take a look around you. Do you know where you are?" Brad seemed more relaxed, perhaps less angry.

"I—" Waldingham's mouth snapped shut suddenly as he felt the pressure of Ving's blunt forefinger in his solar plexus. Ving stared him in the eye, shaking his head no, though he didn't speak. Waldingham seemed to understand.

"You are a member of the embassy staff in Brunei, not Indonesia. You have no authority here, and you've given me no valid reason not to continue with my personal business. I suspect I know who you really work for, and that you have some idea why I'm here. What I don't understand is why you would try to stop me from repatriating a U.S. citizen who has been forcibly abducted and held for ransom."

"You don't have the need to know, Mr. Jacobs, and you would be well advised not to challenge my authority in this matter." Waldingham had regained his voice and his arrogant manner. "I can assure you I will do everything in my power to stop you."

Brad turned to Ving.

"This creep has a bad attitude, Ving, he seems to believe he has the authority to order private citizens around, tell them what they can or can't do in a foreign country."

"Is that so?" Ving said, dead pan. He leaned forward, his eyes inches away from Waldingham's.

"Mr. Waldingham has told me that he is prepared to do everything in his power to keep us from continuing our mission. What do you think of that, Mr. Ving?"

"I think that's downright unsociable, Mr. Jacobs," Ving replied.

"Perhaps we should consider some means of dissuading Mr. Waldingham from pursuing such an ill-advised course of action, Mr. Ving."

"I shall cogitate upon it, Mr. Jacobs. Perhaps I may come up with a non-lethal solution to our dilemma…"

The comic routine mystified Waldingham, Daniel, and Lorenzo, but the people who knew Brad and Ving best were hard put to keep from laughing out loud. Their use of careful diction, combined with Ving's sonorous James Earl Jones voice made the banter sound exactly like the dialogue from and old *Heckle and Jeckle* cartoon.

Ving put a massive hand on Waldingham's shoulder and squeezed hard. He guided Waldingham towards a thick clump of ferns, several yards distant from the others.

"Wait, where are you taking me?" Waldingham spluttered, clearly distressed. Ving squeezed harder, making the attaché flinch and moan. "You can't do this to me!"

"Oh, but we can, Mr. Waldingham," Ving said politely in his basso profundo voice.

"You might have to break his arms, Ving, but don't kill him ... and he's going to need his legs to walk home, so don't break those," Brad called out.

Waldingham yelped in terror.

"Gotcha!"

* * *

As Brad returned to Charlie and the rest of the team, he could hear Daniel trying to explain how he had been coerced.

"Come on, Charlie, you know damned well Detachment 88 is funded and trained by the U.S. Apparently NSA got wind of the fact that Duckworth International Petroleum had been in contact with Team Dallas, but they didn't have the details. They were aware of the kidnapping, but they were totally in the dark as to the identity of the kidnappers or Duckworth's location."

"So how did they get on to you and Lorenzo coming to meet us, Daniel?" Charlie asked evenly.

"I swear to God I don't know, Charlie. All I know is that Waldingham showed up in my department commander's office and he *knew* Charlie. He knew your team had been hired, and he knew they were taking Duckworth to Camp Bashir, though he was calling it Mantiqi III instead of calling it by its proper name."

"So how did he know you were coming here, Daniel?" Brad asked, his face a bland mask.

Daniel's eyes dropped to the ground.

"That's the part I'm truly sorry for. I have to account for my activities on my daily reports, and while I withheld the exact nature of my conversations with Charlie and Lorenzo, I was forced to log the fact that I had spoken with them both. General Lesmarno is a very shrewd man. He connected the dots, and he cornered me in my office. He had everything but physical evidence, sir."

Daniel turned to Charlie, his eyes pleading. "Charlie, you know how it is in the detachment. Tell him." Daniel turned back to Brad. "General Lesmarno does not require actual proof. He is a very intuitive man, and he can be terribly ... persuasive." He looked down at the ground, very close to tears. "I caved."

A terrified cry of pain emanated from the thicket where Ving had taken Waldingham, and the attaché burst out of the flora at a dead run, holding his right arm, gasping, and crying freely. He stumbled and fell to his knees in the dirt. Ving followed him out of the thicket and then past the stricken man to the group, an innocent look on his broad face.

"I believe Mr. Waldingham sees things our way now, though I don't know how long that will last."

"How far is it to the nearest phone?" Brad asked.

"Perhaps twenty kilometers ... back to Sebamban," Daniel answered.

"Ten miles or so?" Ving thought for a moment. "That should give us enough time to get on with our business, Brad—if we take his shoes."

"You are a devious man." Vicky laughed.

"Do it," Brad ordered. Then he watched as Ving, none too gently, relieved Waldingham of his polished wingtip shoes and his socks. When Ving was finished, Brad raised his right hand and waved it in a circle.

"Ass up, people, we're movin'." He spoke to Lorenzo, pointing at Daniel's Humvee. "You drive. I assume you have the weapons stashed nearby?"

Lorenzo nodded.

"Good. Ving, you ride with him. Someone else can pilot your Mrazor for now; I need to have a chat with Daniel."

* * *

Following the Humvee down dusty trails beneath and between impossibly tall trees, Brad made Daniel repeat his account of how Waldingham had come to accompany him to the meeting. After questioning the man repeatedly, Brad accepted his explanation, but he wasn't happy about it.

A half hour after they had left a whining and miserable Waldingham standing in the dirt yard of the burned-out farmhouse, Team Dallas followed the Humvee inside a large, metal barn that Brad suspected was normally used for storing illegal drugs.

Inside, they found a ton-and-a-half crackerbox van and a red and white Cooper Mini parked side by side. Lorenzo opened the back of the van and an armed man sitting inside stepped out. Brad had no choice but to ignore him, though he signaled Jared with his eyes to keep an eye on the gunman.

Lorenzo, once more on familiar, comfortable ground and with a distinct tactical advantage, smiled and waved Brad inside the van. The selection of small arms Lorenzo had brought was small, mostly M-16s, but a quick inspection showed them to be not so badly worn. Brad quickly selected seven of the best looking ones and began breaking them open so that he could check the bolts, the firing pins, trigger mechanisms, and conduct function checks. He had just set the seventh one onto the pile by the overhead door at the back of the van when Lorenzo smiled and reached behind a case of rifles Brad had rejected and came out with a canvas wrapped rifle. He unfolded the canvas and handed the rifle to Brad. The M-16A4 was in pristine condition and had a light coat of LSA lubricant on it. Brad scrutinized it closely, as he had the others, and then checked the ACOG sight.

"Jared!" he called. "Come over here and check this out. I found an old friend of yours."

Jared jogged across the barn and hopped up into the back of the van.

"What've you got, Brad?"

Brad handed him the scoped M-16A4 with its twenty-inch bull barrel, circular forehand guard and flat rail, and the sniper scope.

"Sweet," Jared breathed. "Brings back a lot of memories. Lotta miles totin' one of these."

"I know. Thought you might get a charge out of this. Check it over. If it's good, it's yours."

Jared held the rifle as if it was a lover, and in a very real sense it was. Jared Smoot had been a sniper in Force Recon, but before his days in the elite unit he had been a designated marksman in his squad. He had spent his first five years in the Corps carrying a rifle just like the one he was now holding in his hands.

With movements so quick Brad could scarcely keep up with them, Jared stripped the weapon to its bare bones, inspecting each piece minutely, hefting each part with his eyes closed. To Brad it seemed as if he was watching a Zen master conducting a spiritual ritual to make contact with the soul of the weapon. At length, Jared reassembled the rifle and grunted. Then he adjusted the sling and slung it over his shoulder.

Brad watched in silence as Jared lifted the lid of a footlocker and went through the same ritual with two dozen or more thirty-round magazines before he had accumulated six that were satisfactory to him.

"The others are serviceable," Jared said, grinning. "These are the best.

"Send the others in one at a time," Brad said. "Unless you want a .45. There is a footlocker against the other wall full of them."

"No explosives?"

"I didn't request any. Like we discussed back in Dallas, Jared, this has to be a lightning strike, snatch and run. The mission has to be all about stealth. We can't afford to get into a pitched battle with these people. There are too many variables and no way to determine exactly how many of them there are."

"You're preaching to the choir, Brad. You know me; never take one when you can carry two. It's easier to throw something away than it is to need it and not have it. Just askin'..."

* * *

Lorenzo stood outside the little Cooper Mini, the cash he had gotten from Brad in a canvas bag on the front seat. He had spoken no more than a few sentences the whole time he had been in the presence of the team.

"Nice doing business with you," Brad said, offering to shake hands with the gun dealer.

Lorenzo hesitated then stuck out his hand to shake. When Brad's hand closed around his, Lorenzo felt the power in his grip, and Brad didn't let go.

"My friend Ving here would be very unhappy if word of this transaction were to become known to 'undesirables'," Brad murmured softly, "and I've seen my friend Jared over there, the one with the sniper rifle, take down a Taliban sniper from so far away the guy never heard the sound of the shot. One bullet, right here..." Brad touched a point at the top of Lorenzo's nose, centered in the space between his eyebrows.

Lorenzo smiled a cold smile that didn't touch his eyes.

"If I was that kind of businessman in Indonesia, *bule,* I would be dead already, and if I wanted to take your money and kill you, I would never have collaborated with a member of my country's secret police." Lorenzo fumbled behind him for the door latch on the Mini and backed into the little car, never taking his eyes off Brad or the others. The van had already left. The Cooper started instantly, the sound of the little motor surprisingly powerful inside the barn. In a matter of seconds, the red car was gone.

"Well, that went well," Ving quipped.

TWELVE

When Duckworth first awakened, he thought he was blind. By the time he struggled to a seated position, he realized that his eyes were covered by some kind of cloth. Still groggy and confused, he tried to reach for whatever was covering his eyes, but his hands refused to cooperate. Perplexed, he used his fingers to try to determine why he couldn't separate his hands and discovered that his wrists were fastened together behind him with cold metal bracelets, probably handcuffs.

Panic rose in his chest, and his heart started pounding. The panic threatened to overwhelm him, but he managed to fight it down. He forced himself to take deep breaths until he regained some semblance of control. Once the panic subsided and his breathing returned to normal, he began to take stock of his surroundings.

Even though he could not see, he could sense that he was in a large, enclosed space. The rumbling all around him told him that he was in a large van or truck with hard springs and that it was traveling down a very rough road. He wanted to scream or pound on the walls or floors until someone came to check on him, until the memory of what had happened to him came flooding back into his mind full force.

He remembered his black-clad assailants, small men but very strong, who spoke not a single word nor made a sound when they had snatched him in broad daylight. He had been riding in a spanking new stretch limousine on his way to ink a private agreement with the deputy minister for energy and industry at his private residence. The agreement was to be the culmination of hundreds of hours of work and half a dozen surreptitious negotiations in out of the way spots around the globe. They had gone to great lengths to keep the agreement just between themselves because it was technically, if borderline, illegal. No doubt the sultan would be royally pissed to find out that the deputy minister was lining his own pockets; though, in truth, the deal would be profitable for all concerned. Would have been.

It occurred to Bill that the nature of the private deal must have slipped out somehow, which would explain his current situation. If the government had uncovered evidence of the shady deal, he would have been at best denied entry to the country at the airport. At worst, he would have been met and taken into custody openly by the state police. From what he had read about the island of Borneo, there were several groups of insurgents currently wreaking havoc, most of them militant Islamists. Now he wished he had been more diligent in his research. The stories he had read and seen on the news had painted a gruesome picture in his mind, and as he remembered some of the stories he was forced to fight back a rising panic once again.

There was no way for him to measure the length of time he had spent in the vehicle after he awakened, time was distorted for him in the absolute blackness, and he had no way of knowing how long he had been unconscious. He was aware that his assailants had used chloroform to render him insensible. He could still smell the residue around his nose and mouth and he had a headache from hell. The ride seemed to be lasting forever.

Finally, the truck came to a stop and Duckworth heard shouting in a language that he was totally unfamiliar with. Suddenly, the back door rattled in its tracks as it was raised, and he heard several men climbing into the back. Hands grabbed him and threw him face down on the floor, and then he felt a searing pain in his scalp when someone grabbed a handful of his hair and dragged him out the back of the truck. When he came off the truck, his body slammed onto the ground, his shoulder taking the brunt of the impact. His back arched in agony as one of his unseen assailants kicked at his injured shoulder, causing him to scream.

The beating began in earnest then. Savage, guttural screams sounded all around him as he lay twisting in the dirt, unable to raise his hands from behind his back to protect his face. He felt a boot strike his mouth and blood gushed from his lips. He spluttered and spit out some broken teeth. Duckworth rolled over and scrambled to his knees, ducking his head down and trying as best he could to avoid the rain of vicious blows. Pain blossomed all over his body as the interminable ruthless beating continued, and he began to cry out, begging for it to stop. The only response he got from his pleading was more blows, accompanied by raucous laughter.

Without warning he was roughly jerked to an upright position, still on his knees, and the blindfold was brutally ripped from his head. The brilliant sunlight hurt his eyes so badly that at first he was unable to see. After a few more minutes of beating, he was finally able to see a little, but he still had to squint. He spat, and bright red blood along with shattered fragments of his teeth spread across the dirt in front of him.

Eventually his vision cleared and he could open his eyes wider. Half a dozen men armed with rifles stood around him in a semicircle. They were clad in loose-fitting cotton clothing that had obviously been dyed black. Duckworth noticed that their weapons, at odds with their hand-dyed cotton clothes, were in good condition and coated with a light sheen of oil.

The beating had stopped, and the men were simply staring at him, their rifles at the ready.

"Oh God, no…" he croaked, suddenly certain that they were going to kill him.

The thing that differentiated the leader from the rest of the black-clad hostiles was his impassive hawk-like features and his rigid demeanor. Clearly, he was Middle Eastern instead of Southeast Asian. When he stepped through the line of men haranguing Duckworth, he spoke briefly, but Bill couldn't understand a word the man said. Finally the leader grunted in disgust and barked a few short commands over his shoulder. Instantly two men grabbed Duckworth by the arms and lifted him to his feet. They frog-marched him over to a small, square building with banded steel doors and shoved him inside, slamming the steel door behind him.

* * *

"We have him," the leader said into his satellite phone in perfect American English with no detectable regional accent.

"Did anyone see you take him?" the voice on the other end of the connection asked.

"No, it was clean. Nobody else was around, the troops executed the takedown perfectly, just the way we rehearsed it."

"Good. Everything hinges on keeping him alive, at least until we accomplish our goal, understood?"

"Understood."

"Excellent. Have you checked the satellite link? We have to be absolutely certain they can verify the broadcast is in real time when we put his face on international television."

"We have tested the link twice daily since we arrived. Do not worry, Fadlhan, all is proceeding according to plan."

"No names!" Fadlhan hissed. "How many times do I have to tell you? The cursed Americans are funding and training *Gegana* and we have no way of knowing what kinds of communications technology they have shared with them!"

Ahmad Hamdani scowled into his satellite phone, wondering what Fadlhan had done to earn his spot as team leader on this operation. The man obviously wasn't conversant with modern communications technology; that much was evident. There was no doubt in Hamdani's mind that their communications were being recorded. The question was whether they would ever be heard by human ears. Computers scanned virtually all communications these days, but their search algorithms triggered on keywords. Unless Fadlhan was stupid enough to use Duckworth's name, there was a ninety-nine point nine nine nine percent chance that this conversation would never be heard, and even if it was, there would be no way to trace it back to an exact location. Still, the Imam had placed Fadlhan in charge.

"My mistake," Hamdani said.

"We cannot be too careful now as to our guest. He must remain recognizable, but it's imperative that he appear to have been treated rather badly, you understand?"

Hamdani gritted his teeth in aggravation. They had discussed this part of the plan in minute detail. Duckworth was to be marked up to the point that he was still recognizable but enough that the viewers could see that he had obviously been badly beaten.

"It is done."

"Just make sure that in seven days the bruises are still colorful."

"I was there for the planning stage, I can assure you he will be perfect. Now I must go before we are traced." Hamdani pressed the disconnect button before his anger could get the best of him. Fadlhan was trying his patience.

*   *   *

Bill Duckworth leaned his back against the bare cinder block wall. His face hurt but not as badly as the broken teeth. The two assholes who'd dumped him in this bare cell had not even bothered to remove the handcuffs, but Duckworth had managed to ignore the pain in his shoulder and stomach long enough to slip his feet through his joined hands so that the cuffs were in front of him instead of behind him. It was a small victory, but it made sitting on bare concrete a tiny bit less uncomfortable.

Duckworth was in his mid-fifties, but he kept himself in good shape, working out in his personal gym three days each week and jogging religiously every morning. As a result, he was still functional despite his injuries.

Concentrate Duckworth, he told himself. *Remember everything you've ever read about survival as a hostage.* Bill Duckworth was no fool. The possibility of being taken hostage was an occupational hazard for wealthy Americans who did business abroad. Oil company executives were prime targets, and he had attended several seminars and a couple of week-long training schools to learn as much as he could about the subject. He had been surprised at the amount of information that had been presented, and he had been impressed by some of the guest speakers, who had actually survived being taken hostage. Now, in the blackness of his cell, he couldn't recall if any of the speakers had been taken by Islamic militants.

"Familiarize yourself with your surroundings," he whispered. Despite the pain, he struggled to his knees and began to move along the wall, feeling with his cuffed hands, searching for anything that might be protruding from the wall or hanging from it. "Anything you find that could be used as a weapon or a tool is a possible advantage you cannot afford to ignore." On his first round, the only interruption in the rough cinder block walls was the smooth steel of the door and its frame. The inside of the door was smooth, not even a knob or a lock cylinder protruding from the smooth painted surface. "Pretty slick for a cinder block building built by natives in the middle of a damned rainforest."

The cell was square, about ten feet to a side. No toilet, no water, no windows. He sniffed the air. Not musty but no movement of air. He stood up, hands against the wall, and made the circuit once more, raising his hands as far above his head as he could and downward as far as he could. On the last wall, he found a single screen-covered air vent, but he couldn't detect the slightest trace of light coming in around the edges.

He sank down, sliding his back on the rough wall until his butt settled on the hard concrete. Now, in addition to the injuries inflicted on him by his captors, his knees hurt from crawling on the none-too-clean concrete floor, and his hands were abraded from contact with the cinder block walls. He was hot, and the cell was stuffy. One vent didn't allow for good airflow, even though it allowed oxygen to enter. He drew his knees up and leaned forward, his face resting in his sore hands. There was nothing he could use, nothing that would give him the slightest advantage.

Bill Duckworth made his first real error. He felt black despair tugging at his soul. No one at D.I.P. even knew he had gone to Brunei. He had carefully covered his tracks so that his staff and his family believed that he was in Fiji on an executive retreat, not to be disturbed. By now he supposed someone at home knew he had been taken, the terrorists would have taken care of that, but they wouldn't know where he had been taken to. He didn't even know himself. He let the despair wash over him, and he began to cry.

* * *

The sound of the door hinges startled him awake. The figure of a man, indistinguishable in the dark, stood outlined in the doorway. It must have been dark outside because there was only enough light to expose the man's outline in the door opening.

Duckworth watched as the man silently squatted down, setting something on the floor. Standing up, the man backed slowly out the door and shut it without ever having uttered a sound. Alone again.

For a moment Duckworth sat in the silence, just listening. He knew where the vent was located though he couldn't see it. His ears strained to hear any sound that might give him a clue about anything at all. He was able to distinguish some sounds he thought might be insects, but they weren't any insects he had ever heard before. He heard what might have been muffled laughter, but he couldn't be certain it wasn't an animal. *Have they left me alone here? There's at least one, I saw him! But where the hell are the others?* For the first time, he wondered if he had made the wrong assumptions. Could it be that he had it wrong? Did they want something other than ransom money?

He crawled over to the doorway and felt around in the darkness until his hands closed on a thick paper plate. His fingers sank into something greasy and unpleasant. He raised his fingers to his nose. It smelled vile. Putting his hands down again in disgust, he explored until he encountered a small paper cup, which he almost knocked over before he could save it. Raising the cup to his nose, he sniffed again. There was nothing in the aroma that smelled of chemicals or poison, but it was none too clean. He could deal with hunger, even though all the seminars had emphasized eating whatever was given because maintaining your strength was critical. He knew he could not do without water. He was still sweating.

Though the cinder block walls were cool to the touch, the ambient air was muggy and hot. He sipped from the cup, taking a small amount into his mouth and swishing it around. The soft tissues inside his mouth absorbed the greasy moisture even as the taste made him gag. Twice more he repeated the sip and swish routine, gagging both times. Finally, he raised the cup again and drained it. His stomach rebelled, but he managed to hold it down.

* * *

"Ibrahim, did the *bule* eat?"

"I do not know for certain, *tuan* (sir), the infrared images are not as clear as I'd like. I know he picked up the paper plate."

"Did he drink?"

"Yes *Tuan*, at least I think so, he raised the cup to his lips several times."

"Good. I am not concerned about the food, but we need him alive for the time being. Next time, give him clean water, but be sure the food is barely edible, and take him out into the light tomorrow. If he has fouled himself, hose him down. If the bruises have not begun to color, beat him some more. We need him to appear battered when we take him before the cameras next week."

Ibrahim acknowledged his understanding with a nod and took his leave as quickly as he deemed polite. He was nominally in charge of Camp Bashir and the training program, but it had been made clear to him by his superiors that Hamdani's instructions were to be followed to the letter in all things pertaining to the hostage. The decision to bring the hostage to Camp Bashir had been a bad one as far as Ibrahim was concerned. It had taxed his training resources to the limit, causing an interruption in the training schedule, and he was worried that it would draw attention to the carefully hidden facility. Jemaah Islamiyah had worked long and hard to get the political concessions that kept the government away from the area, and a high profile hostage's presence could well draw the attention of other nations' intelligence agencies and compromise the integrity of the training site.

He sighed heavily as he stepped outside the residence assigned to Hamdani for the length of his stay. Orders were orders, however distasteful, and he would obey them to the best of his ability. The only positive aspect he could see to the entire operation was the monstrous amount of money the cause would receive when the ransom was paid. A great deal could be accomplished with a hundred million dollars, and it would bring JI so much closer to establishing the caliphate in Southeast Asia ... and that justified the risks involved. If everything went according to plan, the lunacy would be over in seven short days and he would be rid of Hamdani and the hostage both. The end couldn't come soon enough to suit him.

THIRTEEN

The going was fairly easy at first. The two Mrazors sped down unimproved roads for a very short time until Brad pulled off onto a rutted logging trail shooting off the roadway at the apex of a sharp curve and shut down his machine. He removed one of the maps Herb had given him and used his finger to trace the path they had taken from the beach to the contact point and from there to the spot where he had turned off the unimproved road. The logging trail wasn't marked. He took out his satellite phone to check their coordinates on the GPS. The team had left their BlackBerries in the baggage they had stashed on Louise because Charlie had told them that cell phone service was sporadic in parts of the Kalimantan interior.

Ving shut down his machine and got out to peer at the map with Brad.

"Wish Herb had covered this thing with acetate," he grumped. "If that thing gets wet, we're screwed."

Brad compared the position he had plotted on the map by terrain association with the coordinates from the GPS and was pleased to note that they were the same.

"From what I can see of the terrain, this logging trail should follow this ridgeline most of the way to this pass." His forefinger pointed to the pass Charlie had told him led to the unimproved road that terminated in the camp.

"Rough going between here and there, Brad," Charlie commented. He had gone into the brush to relieve himself before joining the others at the front of Brad's Mrazor. He stared down at the map spread over the slanted hood. "We can only hope the water's not up on these intermittent streams. If there's been rainfall up in the mountains, which is likely this time of year, we're going to have a little trouble fording them." He paused then slid his finger over to a river. "As I recall, this is fordable right about here. Daniel and I were on foot, so we didn't have to worry about getting a vehicle across, but it was no more than waist deep so we waded. If the river is up, we may have to swim across and use the winches to pull us."

"Yeah, I remember you telling me that, that's why we ordered the snorkels and winches. We're gonna get wet, no doubt about it, but we don't want to take the chance of being detected by checkpoints or lookouts along the access road leading out of the camp. I'm hoping these things are as fast as advertised, though, otherwise our extraction plan is for shit, Charlie."

"We should check the speed out before we go off-road, Brad. It would be a helluva downer to find out they ain't fast enough when we're trying to run a gauntlet of pissed off jihadists," Ving said thoughtfully.

Brad thought for a moment before nodding his head in agreement. "Too much stuff I didn't think through going into this mission," he muttered ruefully.

Vicky, sensing his concern, touched his arm lightly.

"You've done a good job so far, Brad. Don't start doubting yourself now."

"Plenty of time to rethink things on the way to the objective, Brad," Jared drawled, climbing into Ving's Mrazor. "Let's get this circus on the road." He grinned. "Come on, Pete, if this thing can hit sixty with your big ass and Ving's in here at the same time, we're good."

"Smart ass!" Ving said good-naturedly as he and Pete climbed into the vehicle. He cranked the engine and spun the Mrazor around, driving it back onto the dirt road and flooring the accelerator. The turbocharger whined as it kicked in and a cloud of dust rose in the air behind it.

"Just as well check both of them," Brad said, motioning for the others to load up. In seconds they were blasting down the dirt road behind Ving. The Mrazors were fast.

* * *

The logging trail wound in and out but continued in the same general direction the team needed to go. Brad, in the lead vehicle, stopped whenever he was unsure of the general direction they were traveling and checked their position using both the map and the GPS. Even though they had traveled a farther distance on the winding trail than they would have on foot in a straight line, their progress was much faster because of the speed of the Mrazors. The trail was so bad in places that they were amazed that logging vehicles had managed to negotiate it.

Jessica finally remarked on it. "I can't believe they get big, old logging trucks through this mess," she said as they splashed through a particularly muddy section of trail.

"They don't," Charlie said, laughing. "This is the interior of South Kalimantan. Labor is dirt cheap here. The loggers pick up day laborers from isolated villages and bring them to the logging camps. From there they walk to the harvesting sites and harness them to chains and drag the logs out to where they can be lifted onto the trucks. When they are cutting the really big logs, they use teams of oxen to drag the logs out to where the trucks can access them. Some Shorea tree trunks are so huge they have to use several teams of oxen, and the laborers have to fell smaller trees to clear a path. It's a lot of effort, but there is a huge market for the giant logs and they bring a hell of a price."

"I still don't see how they get the logging trucks down any of these trails, Charlie," Jessica said. "All these switchbacks and sharp turns…"

"We haven't reached one of the truck trails yet, Jess. Watch for big clearings where they set up temporary sawmills. We'll see better trails then." He hesitated for a moment. "Most of the logging on this side of the mountains is illegal. The loggers go to a great deal of effort to conceal their access routes, and it's the wrong time of year for logging anyway."

"What do you mean, 'the wrong time of year'?" Jessica asked.

"It's the rainy season."

As if on cue, rain began to fall, great waves of rain, and the trail quickly became a soupy morass. The Mrazors kept moving, though their progress slowed considerably and the wide lugs of the off-road tires slung gouts of mud high into the air. In no time the team was coated with dark, slimy mud.

* * *

The logging trail had become all but impassable, and Brad had rolled off to one side beneath the limited cover of one of the great Shorea trees. He had placed the folded up map inside a cheap, disposable plastic poncho that he'd picked up as an afterthought at a dollar store back in Dallas. None of them had bothered to take their rain gear from their backpacks until they were already soaked and covered with mud.

"We need to get off the trail now and go straight for the pass," Brad muttered. "We went too far north on that last leg." He turned to Vicky and Jess, who were both busy scraping the black mud of the trail from their clothing. "You might want to dig out your ponchos now."

"Fat lot of good they will do now," Jessica growled. "I've got mud in places I can't even talk about in mixed company!"

Vicky laughed. She had tied her hair into a ponytail early on and wrapped a bandana around her face.

"We can clean up later. It's just as likely we're going to run into dusty roads on the other side of that pass. According to what I read, the weather here changes every fifteen minutes."

Ignoring the byplay between the two women, Charlie leaned over the map, trying to read it through the semi-transparent plastic of the poncho.

"We can go ahead this way, northwards, but it's going to get rugged," he said, running his finger along a draw running straight west. "It's for damned sure gonna get wetter though." He looked up at the angry clouds above them. "There's gonna be 'intermittent' streams in all the low spots and the ridgeline is going to be all but impassable because its slopes are so steep." The contour intervals on the map were so close together that they almost looked like a single solid brown line.

"We can't take a chance on the logging trail doubling back," Jared pointed out. "Looks like a drop-off coming up on the west side of the route we've been following, and the trail has been following the high ground."

They loaded up and moved on, striking straight west or at least as straight as they were able. Charlie proved correct in his assumption. The Mrazors had progressed less than two hundred yards before they encountered a stream. Pete, wielding a heavy machete he'd strapped to the back of his rucksack, chopped down a sapling about two inches in diameter and ten feet long. He handed the machete back to Ving and then walked around the front of the first Mrazor and cautiously waded into the swiftly moving muddy water, using the sapling as a probe to check the depth of the water and to search for obstacles. When he got to the far side, he turned and waved for the vehicles to come across.

Brad eased the front wheels into the swiftly moving water, unsure of how the Mrazor was going to behave when fording, and he thought his heart would stop when he felt the wheels begin to spin as the water crept up to his knees. His confidence began to return as the vehicle lurched as the tires caught and climbed slowly out the other side and onto relatively dry land.

Ving yelled, "Hang on!" and hit the water at full speed once Brad was clear. Jared grinned and grabbed hold of the roll bar as they splashed into the water. The Mrazor never bogged down, it pushed through the water, barely slowing, and popped out the other side.

The terrain was even rougher than Brad had imagined, but the Mrazors were handling it incredibly well. Occasionally they were forced to stop and hack down a sapling, and once they were forced to hack their way through a seemingly endless bamboo thicket. It was backbreaking work, and at one point Jessica, who was taking her turn with the machete, encountered a coiled and angry denizen of the thicket. Under the admiring eyes of the team, she dispatched the angry serpent with a quick downstroke of the machete and continued chopping.

The rain stopped just before midnight, and the moonlight shone through the cloud cover. The temperature, which had dropped to a balmy eighty-odd degrees, began to rise. The humidity was awful, and the insects emerged to feed. The Mrazors were moving so slowly in the dark that the insects were able to dine on Team Dallas. They were suddenly glad of the mud that covered them. An hour or so after the rain stopped, Brad's Mrazor came to a stop on the bank of a swollen river. Both Mrazors shut down, and the team gathered at the edge of the water.

"Looks deep as hell to me," Jared said.

Pete bent down and picked up a stick, shaving the bark off the outside with his razor sharp boot knife until the inner wood gleamed softly in the pale moonlight. The others watched curiously as he slipped the knife back into the sheath in his boot and then tossed the stick upstream. The stick swept past them with surprising speed.

"Looks deep and it's moving fast. We need to look for a better place to ford, Brad. If we try to go in here we're gonna be screwed."

"It's dark and there's no way we can reach Camp Bashir tonight," Charlie murmured.

"We can't stop now," Brad said decisively. He glanced down and peeled the Velcro cover from over the face of his radium dial chronometer. "Duckworth has been in captivity for five days now, and we are dangerously close to the first deadline set by the kidnappers."

"I thought Mr. Grainger told you his committee had negotiated an extra week," Vicky commented.

"He did, but something has been nagging at me from the beginning. I'll be honest, I don't know what it is, but something doesn't feel right."

"Then why did we take this contract, Brad?" Vicky wasn't being critical; she was asking him a legitimate question in a non-challenging way.

"Because I established the fact that an American citizen had been kidnapped and needed our help. Because I have a distinct lack of confidence in ex-C.I.A. employees and I got the distinct impression from our visitor on the beach that I was right in assuming that there is more at play here than meets the eye. 'Cultural Attaché' my ass. The Company doesn't want us involved in this, and I want to know why."

No one had a response to that; they all wondered what the C.I.A. involvement was. Not one of them was comfortable with the idea that someone was trying to play Team Dallas, especially the C.I.A.

Brad faced his team.

"I admit I have some misgivings. I should have spoken up before now that's for damned sure." He paused to wipe the sweat from his eyes. "This is what I'm going to do. I'm gonna go to the left, search for a place we can ford. Jared, you take the right. If you can't find a spot within five hundred meters, call me on your sat phone and come on back to the Mrazors. Unless I get a call on my sat phone saying you've found a ford or that you're coming back, I'm gonna keep going till I find a ford or a bridge.

"I want the rest of you to check and clean your weapons. Make sure you're locked and loaded. Use the time to think, people. Anybody who wants to tap out when I get back is free to do so, no questions asked and no blame attached." The speech was longer than he'd intended, but it came from the heart. Shouldering his M-16 and patting his hip to make sure the .45 he'd selected was still secure in its holster, he headed downstream, paralleling the bank of the river.

* * *

Brad had located a shallow ford within two hundred meters, a spot where the river spread out and got shallower. He waded out into the water and was pleased to find that there was a substantial bed of gravel beneath the surface. It was a man-made improvement that told him a logging company had used the ford at one time or another, though any trace of the old logging road had long since been overgrown. He pulled out his sat phone and recalled Jared then made his way back to the Mrazors.

His return to the vehicles took very little time. The team, every member, stood in a semicircle around the south side of the vehicles. Brad came to a full stop ten feet away.

"Well?" he asked.

"It's a little insultin', you feelin' like you had ta ask, Brad," Jared said in his slow Texas drawl.

"We're in, Brad, all of us." Vicky, tall, slim, and covered in mud, spoke softly and clearly over the hum of the insects, which were growing more insistent on devouring Team Dallas by the second.

* * *

The heat was terrific and the insects almost unbearable when the sun rose above the horizon. Somewhere around midmorning they were well up the slopes of the first of the mountains of the range leading to the valley where Camp Bashir was located. Brad called a halt to check their position and see how far they had to go before they reached their objective. The map, damp and slightly smeared, was spread across the hood of the lead Mrazor, while Brad, sat phone in hand, pored over it plotting their location by the GPS coordinates.

"What the…?" Ving exclaimed, his head tilted back, his eyes scanning the skies.

"Shit!" Pete and the others were all staring upward and Brad finally realized that he had been far too focused on the map. Off in the distance he could hear the unmistakable 'flucketa-flucketa' sound made by the rotors of a low flying UH-1 Huey. There was no way to tell from which direction the chopper was coming, the sound seemed to come from all around them and was growing louder by the second.

"Camouflage the vehicles!" Brad barked. The team rushed to gather ferns and palmetto fronds, which they placed primarily over the tops of the Mrazors to disguise them from above.

"That should be enough; we just needed to break up the outlines. Get under cover, quick!" Brad shoved Vicky toward a cluster of palmetto plants and they dove beneath the fronds just as the chopper flashed overhead.

The chopper was an old Huey, painted flat black with no visible markings. Brad was about to breathe a sigh of relief when the chopper banked steeply and headed back over their position.

"Shit!" Brad muttered again. He craned his neck up to get a better look at the bird as it flew overhead again. This time he could clearly see a gunner in the open door. Right beside the gunner, leaning out the open door and peering down intently at the ground was Lawrence P. Waldingham III. His left arm was in a sling.

The chopper passed over them slowly, going back the way it had come from. As the sound of the rotors faded away to nothing and they were left with only the sounds of the rainforest, everyone crawled out into the open.

"Son of a bitch!" Ving fumed. He faced Brad. "I shoulda broke his legs when I had the chance!"

"That puts a wrinkle in our plans," Brad mused. "I don't think that chopper had thermal imaging gear, otherwise that door gunner would have shredded us right here."

"That bird didn't have any of the external sensors, cameras or antennae needed to operate advanced thermal imaging or advanced detection systems," Pete said. "That baby was stripped down to the bone."

"I know the Company doesn't want us here, but you don't really believe they're really willing to kill us, do you?" Jessica asked. "I mean they wouldn't really murder U.S. citizens in cold blood…"

"Two things," Vicky interjected, "the first is that you can never tell with the Agency. They operate under their own rules. The second is that we aren't in the U.S.; we're in the middle of the South Kalimantan rainforest. If they greased us out here, in all likelihood no one would ever find our bodies. Anything they do out here is plausibly deniable."

"True," said Charlie. "We have no embassy in Kalimantan, and when I was out here before, Daniel told me the airspace here is restricted. JI has a lock on the local government, even the Indonesian police and military aren't permitted to fly here."

Jared stroked his chin thoughtfully. "I don't think they're ready to eliminate us just yet … and I'm not as certain as you are that they didn't spot us, Brad."

Ving spoke up. "I'm thinkin' Jared has a point. If they'd a wanted us dead, they coulda saved themselves a whole passel of trouble by smokin' us on the beach."

"If you've got it right, Ving, they'll be back soon … with help."

"Don't be too sure they'll have help, Brad," Charlie said. "Waldingham is down here on his own. If he'd had backup, they would have been close by when he met us on the beach. I'm guessing he's called for backup, but they'd have to be coming from Brunei. He must have gotten someone to pick him up on the road back to Sebamban and get him to a telephone or he never would have gotten a chopper here this fast."

"I'd like to know how he got a chopper here at all! As far as I know a Huey only has a range of about three hundred miles ... and that would mean he had support inside Indonesia."

"No Ving, those pods mounted off the skids were auxiliary fuel tanks and they give them at least double the range," Pete said. "He'd have to have a fuel re-supply point in country though. Charlie, where the hell would the C.I.A. keep a covert helicopter around here?"

"I've heard rumors of a black team in Sarawak (Malaysia) Pete, around six hundred miles from here as the crow flies, but I never got confirmation…"

Track Down Borneo

Brad put his hands to his head, focusing, concentrating. Finally, he lifted his head, confident and fully in charge once more.

"We have to assume that by now the C.I.A. has assets on the ground nearby. I think we have to assume that Waldingham saw *something* that told him we were here and that he's had to go back and refuel, especially if he's been tracking us all the way from where we left him."

"What I don't get is why they're using a Huey at all man. That is some *old* ass hardware. The C.I.A. ain't short of funds. Why ain't Waldingham ridin' a Blackhawk?"

"I have an idea," Vicky said slowly. "What if the op they're running isn't sanctioned? What if they're paying for this out of some sort of 'off the books' slush fund?"

Everyone thought *that* over for a few minutes.

"Strip off the camouflage," Brad said decisively. "We need to get as far away from this spot as we can as fast as we can move. If we push it and we have a little luck, by the time Waldingham can get back out here to continue his search, we will be most of the way to Camp Bashir and he'll have a helluva time picking up our trail. At nightfall we slow down again. I don't want to alert the kidnappers, so we go stealth mode when we get within twenty klicks." He paused for breath. "Ass up, people, we're moving!"

FOURTEEN

Ahmad Hamdani had been appointed commander at Camp Bashir over Amir Ibrahim, the chief training instructor, at least for the duration of the current operation. He had joined Jemaah Islamiyah in 1996 after Osama bin Laden had been expelled from Sudan and sought refuge in Afghanistan. His aggressive, warlike nature had been recognized early on by his superiors and he had been specially selected and sent to Afghanistan with two Malaysian men: Zulkifli Abdhir, also known as 'Marwan', who had studied engineering in the U.S., and Dr. Azahari bin Husin, who later became known as "Demolition Man", for training in the fine art of making bombs. Husin eventually wrote the JI bomb manual.

Hamdani, over the years, had been utilized in Afghanistan, Jakarta, Bali, Yemen, Sudan, Ethiopia, and even in the United States. Eventually he had been seconded to *Mantiqi III* to train the next generation.

Hamdani, it turned out, had an extraordinary natural talent for managing the headstrong youths that were drawn to and recruited by Jemaah Islamiyah. His skill and abilities had been quickly recognized by the head of his *wakalah*, then the head of his *mantiqi*, and eventually by Abu Bakar Bashir, the cofounder of Jemaah Islamiyah. Even with his exceptional abilities, however, he found it difficult at times to control his young charges.

The acolytes, eager to serve the cause of jihad, were prone to get carried away when they executed even a training mission. More often than not this resulted in the deaths of people that Hamdani did not wish to be killed. He was particularly concerned with the welfare of his current hostage, William Duckworth, because of the unusual conditions imposed by the high ranking Fadlhan, who had been sent down to

Camp Bashir from the headquarters element of *Mantiqi III* especially to instruct Hamdani on the handling of the hostage.

In all the years he had served the cause, he had never seen a hostage treated as he had been commanded to handle Duckworth. Hostages had never been coddled or given more than the bare necessities; that was a part of the rigorous program of psychological conditioning and religious instruction meted out to all captives of Jemaah Islamiyah to keep them docile and malleable. Hamdani had never before been ordered to 'mark' a hostage up in a precise manner for a camera appearance, and he found the practice somehow distasteful. He was not overly fond of the arrogant Fadlhan either.

Duckworth was particularly hated by the trainees because he was perceived as an exploiter of the faithful as well as an infidel, and it had taken all of Hamdani's skill as a leader to keep them from killing him out of hand. Fadlhan's instructions were explicit; Duckworth was to be kept alive at all costs, but he was to plainly exhibit the marks of having been beaten and abused. The tactic was very similar to what Hamdani had seen and disapproved of in Afghanistan. His time there had been long and unpleasant, as the Taliban were hard and cruel beyond belief. They professed to be followers of the Prophet, all praise to him, but they did not adhere to his teaching. Beheading was a punishment decreed by the Quran and thus sanctified. Torture, which the Afghans seemed to relish, was not a practice endorsed by the faith.

Unlike many of the renegade cell leaders associated with the local *wakalah*, Hamdani was acutely aware of Jemaah Islamiyah's strategy, one adopted from U.S. military strategy, the winning of the hearts and minds of the people of Indonesia. The ransom money Duckworth would bring would allow Jemaah Islamiyah to provide and distribute much needed food, medical care, and supplies to the poor and disenfranchised of Kalimantan. The ransom of William Darnell Duckworth IV was a critical assignment he dared not screw up.

In order to keep Duckworth safe, Hamdani had restricted access to the hostage to the most seasoned and experienced of his training cadre. Distracting the overeager trainees required a great deal of effort and thought, had delayed the training program, and would set it back indefinitely. A minimum guard of experienced cadre kept watch on the small cinderblock building where Duckworth was held, leaving a handful of experienced men to conduct the constant field training exercises Hamdani had hastily planned to keep the trainees' hostile attentions off him. The training was especially designed to keep the trainees occupied day and night. Hamdani had managed to salvage some training value from the exercises because it was teaching his subordinate leaders how to control the overeager recruits.

As a concession to the youngsters' over exuberance—and to distract them from the presence of Duckworth—Hamdani had allowed them live ammunition and planned for live fire training in the remote and sparsely populated areas in the mountains surrounding the valley. There was still the risk of unwanted deaths because the interior of South Kalimantan was populated sparsely by the Dayak (the indigenous people of Kalimantan who were predominantly non-Muslim) villages. The Dayak collected cash crops from the rainforest, which they considered to be their land, and sold them in the coastal markets. Not a particularly peaceful people, the Dayak were the original headhunters of Borneo.

Hamdani fervently believed that the ransom money would be worth the risks involved, and he doubted that the tenuous unspoken agreement between *Mantiqi III* and the government of South Kalimantan would be affected by the deaths of a few Dayak. The Dayak had never been able to get along with the government anyway; they were generally left to their own devices and had little interaction with the government.

* * *

Amir Ibrahim controlled the patrol of recruits from behind the center of the group, constantly on the alert for stragglers. Having a raw recruit behind him with a loaded weapon was not an idea he was comfortable with. He kept the group on line about fifteen paces ahead of him, using voice commands to guide the inexperienced group. Later, when they had grasped the concepts he was trying to teach them, he would switch to the hand signals that they had not yet become familiar with. His personal opinion was that Hamdani had lost his mind; sending the recruits into the mountains in terrain that was difficult at best with weapons and live ammunition was foolish. Sending them at night in the rainy season was insane.

Ibrahim, son of a Javanese mother and an Arab father, had grown up in a family totally committed to the idea of establishing a caliphate in Southeast Asia, centered in their homeland. His father had settled in Jakarta after meeting and marrying his mother. His father had been martyred on December 18, 1998 in a clash between security forces on the island of Basilan and Abu Sayyaf. Ibrahim's mother had then sent her son to Afghanistan to train with the fledgling Al-Qaeda so that he could eventually avenge his father's death.

Over the intervening years Ibrahim had fought in Syria, Sudan, Yemen, Ethiopia, anywhere there was fighting. He'd learned his trade well, and he'd eventually returned home to Indonesia and Jemaah Islamiyah. Now he was marching around on the steep slopes of a mountain in South Kalimantan behind a bunch of raw recruits with loaded weapons. His only consolation was that if he was killed this night it would be by accident instead of on purpose.

"Halt!" he called out in a stentorian voice, raising his clenched fist above his head in the signal for a halt, just to familiarize them with the command. "Weapons to the front, remove your magazines!" He swept the long line, his hawk-like eyes searching for someone foolish enough to turn around with their weapon pointing to the rear. It had happened twice already on this exercise, and he had promptly disciplined the hapless offender by applying the butt of his own M-16 to the boy's chin. Not full force but hard enough to make an impression. "Lock your bolts to the rear!"

Ibrahim heard the sound of a bolt slamming forward, followed by the sound of a single round going off.

"Freeze!" he shouted, making his way towards the right side of the line where a shamefaced seventeen-year-old was flinching in anticipation of the punishment to come. Ibrahim didn't say a word, he just butt-stroked the kid in the back of the head, sending him sprawling, unconscious, to the ground. After a moment, the recruit that had been standing next to the offender started to kneel down to check on his fallen comrade.

"Leave him!" Ibrahim commanded. "If he wakes up, he will know better next time. Take this as an object lesson—do not put a round in your chamber until I tell you to. He might have killed or seriously wounded any one of you because he stupidly disobeyed my direct order. There is no glory and no reward for dying of stupidity. Save your lives for Allah, praise be his name." He looked down at the fallen recruit. *"Blo'on,"* (idiot) he muttered under his breath.

"Break down into your *regu* (squads). We will eat here and break for an hour."

The recruits broke down into squads of five each and began to scrabble about for materials dry enough for a small cook fire. They carried coffee or tea, and most ate *tempe* (fried fermented soy bean patty) and balls of precooked rice. A few used their canteen cups to make *rami* (ramen noodles).

Ibrahim separated himself from the recruits and moved off about thirty paces from the others, where the seven cadre members who were assisting him with the training were already building a small communal fire to share with him. *"Blo'on,"* he repeated as he squatted down by the fire. None of the cadre members looked up.

FIFTEEN

Brad was extremely impressed with the performance of the Mrazors. The pass they were heading for was a high one, more of a saddle between two peaks. Climbing for the pass was far less difficult than climbing the mountain itself, but it wasn't easy by any means. As they hurried up the slope towards the saddle, the team was frequently forced to detour around the thickest part of the underbrush or utilize footpaths and trails. The use of their GPS capability, combined the incredible speed of the Mrazors, more than made up for the time they lost in the detours.

Brad held up a hand as he came to a halt at a steep ravine, apparently the result of volcanic activity eons before.

"Dammit! This isn't on the map!" he muttered. He pulled out his satellite phone and double-checked their position on the map. "If we have to double back, we're going to lose half a day," he grumbled.

Vicky craned her neck, looking for some way around the obstacle, but there was nothing. One end of the ravine opened over a sheer drop of several hundred feet. The other end terminated in a vertical wall rising straight up about ninety feet.

Ving had climbed out of his Mrazor and walked around to peer into the ravine.

"That's at least a twenty-degree slope," he muttered. "No way these things are gonna be able to negotiate that with a load."

"That's what the winch is for, guys," Jared said, reaching for the hook on the end of the winch cable. "We hook this around one of these trees and back down, then we winch the Mrazor up the other side."

Brad peered across the ravine, estimating the opposite slope's angle and height.

"It's climbable," he said. "Come on, let's do it. We're running too far behind as it is."

Jared and Pete wrapped the cable around the base of a massive Shorea tree while Brad reversed the Mrazor, backing to within inches of the downslope.

"You're going to have to ride it down, Brad. The control is mounted on the console inside the cockpit." Jessica was smiling at him, amused at the look on Brad's face.

"Very funny," he responded. "I hate this." He slipped the machine into gear and edged back over the rim of the ravine; Jared, one hand on the back of the roll cage, slipped and slid as the Mrazor inched toward the bottom of the ravine.

"I don't want to be anywhere close to that thing if the cable breaks," Jessica remarked, glancing at Vicky. "I think we should take our chances on a free climb."

"Oh for pity's sake, Jess, it's not that steep," Vicky retorted as she stepped over the edge and carefully began to negotiate the slope. What was impossible for a machine was not that difficult for a human.

"I was kidding, Vicky," Jessica said with a laugh. She stepped down onto the slope and beat Vicky to the bottom.

"I'll hook you up, Ving, and stay up here to release the cables when you're down," Pete said, grasping the cable from the front of the second Mrazor and waiting for Ving to trigger the release.

* * *

The mud from the previous day had in large part dried and cracked off their clothing, leaving it crusty and stiff. The downslope of the ravine had proved to be more slippery than it first appeared, and only Jessica, Brad, and Ving reached the bottom relatively clean. The others were wearing a fresh coat of clay. Wordlessly, Jared took the cable ends from Pete and began to ascend the far side.

The ascent of the far side was much slower, and Brad was forced to use every ounce of the turbo diesel's power to clear the last few feet because both Vicky and Jessica were clinging to the roll cage. The upslope had been considerably slippier than the opposite side.

Charlie had reluctantly grabbed onto the roll cage of Ving's Mrazor for an assist, but Pete had stubbornly insisted on making the steep climb on his own. By the time the team had climbed out of the ravine and rested for a few minutes, it was well past noon.

"We've got to get moving. This is taking far longer than we planned, and the clock is running down for Duckworth..."

"I'm just hopin' Herb doesn't bail on us, Brad," Jared said.

"Yeah, it'd be a hell of a thing to get all the way back to the beach with Duckworth and not have a ride home," Ving remarked. He chuckled after he made the statement, but Brad could tell there was real concern in his voice.

"The contract calls for him to give us up to seventy-two hours, and I've got his sat phone number on speed dial," Vicky said flatly.

"We all know there's no such thing as an op going off exactly as planned, people. I get nervous when everything goes just the way I planned it and there were a lot of loose ends on this mission to start with. Improvise, adapt, overcome, remember?" Brad spoke with more confidence than he felt. There *had* been a lot of loose ends to prepare for on this mission, and he *had* made some leaps of faith in planning the mission, something he ordinarily would have never allowed himself to consider. He had allowed himself to be distracted by Willona's glowing plans for the business and his growing enthusiasm for her ideas as he came to see the possibilities. He was ashamed to admit that he had been so excited by the prospect of the enormous fee that Willona had negotiated that he had permitted avarice to cloud his professional judgment ... and now Team Dallas and Duckworth might have to pay the cost. Now the rosy future was dependent upon his ability to do what he had always done—accomplish his mission and bring his team back alive.

"Saddle up, people," he said with new resolve, "we have a hostage to rescue."

* * *

Within an hour they came to a spot in the rainforest that had obviously been clear-cut and then replanted with oil palms. The oil palms were not native to Borneo; rather, they had been imported to the island from Africa to be used as a quick cash crop. Large plantations of the tree had been built in more populous areas of the rainforest, but they had come under increasing pressure in recent years from environmentalists and the medical community ... and that had opened a window of opportunity for the Dayak and other tribes in the interior.

Brad brought the lead Mrazor to a halt and shut down the engine at the leading edge of the space, visually surveying the area for threats. The irregularly shaped field was not large, perhaps a hundred yards deep and fifty wide. Charlie, in the second row of seats in the Mrazor beside Jessica, spoke up uneasily.

"The Dayak have these fields scattered through the mountains. It's best not to stick around them any more than you have to. You can never tell when you might meet up with them ... and they can get hostile with outsiders."

"We won't be here any longer than absolutely necessary, and we're not looking for trouble."

"Doesn't matter if we're looking for trouble, Brad. These guys are the original headhunters of Borneo—literally. It was some part of their religious beliefs, and I'm reliably informed that some backcountry tribes still practice the art of shrinking the heads of their enemies."

Jessica shifted in her seat, easing her M-16 into a ready position and curling her hand tightly around the pistol grip. She wasn't afraid, just cautious. Facing pygmies in Africa hadn't fazed her, but she wasn't the type to let her guard down easily. If they encountered hostiles, she would hold her own.

As if on cue, a group of three natives came out of the rainforest and into the far end of the field carrying oil palm chisels and sickles. Working tools were not all they carried. Each of them had an M-16 slung across their backs. The team held their collective breaths as the Dayak spread out into the field, checking the oil palms for bunches of ripe fruit. One of them turned to walk up the row of trees that led to them and instantly cried out a guttural warning. His tools dropped to the ground and his M-16 appeared in his hands as if by magic. Just as swiftly the other two were transformed from peaceful harvesters to defenders of the tribal field.

Brad wasn't sure what he'd expected, but the fierce-looking men approaching him in khaki bush shorts were not it. Their bodies were marked with large tribal tattoos, but they were not adorned with bone necklaces and earrings. They wore bright red headbands around their arrow-straight, jet-black hair and each had a machete in a sheath suspended from their waist. Barefoot, they spread out, approaching Team Dallas. They seemed as natural and comfortable with the rifles as they had with their chisels and sickles.

"Don't make any sudden moves," Charlie muttered.

"Charlie," Jessica whispered, "shouldn't we—"

"If they were going to attack us, they'd already be shooting, Jess …"

"He's right, don't make any sudden moves," Brad whispered out the side of his mouth.

Ving noticed Jared easing the safety switch off on his M-16 and silently cursed himself for slinging his own onto the carrier on the Mrazor's roll cage. As inconspicuously as possible, he began to ease the .45 in its holster, leaving his big hand resting on the grip.

"Don't say anything, Brad," Charlie whispered. "If there's any talking to be done, let him do it." Charlie slowly raised his hands to show he held no weapons. Praying that Ving and Jared could cover them if it became necessary, Brad raised his hands as well.

The tallest of the Dayak stopped about twenty yards away, his rifle leveled at Brad.

"Tinggalkan tempat ini." He waved the barrel of the M-16 menacingly, indicating the rainforest. When Brad showed no sign of understanding what had been said, the other two Dayak raised their weapons as well and the tallest, apparently the leader, shook the barrel of his weapon at Brad again. *"Pergi sekarang!"* Once more he swept the barrel of his rifle in the direction of the rainforest.

"I think he's telling us to get the hell out of Dodge," Brad muttered.

"I don't speak the lingo either," Jared drawled from the rear Mrazor, "but I'm inclined to agree with you."

"Don't have to tell me twice," Ving muttered and then pushed the starter button on the dashboard. Brad refused to start his until Ving was moving.

"Don't go fast," he ordered. He whispered again out of the corner of his mouth, addressing his passengers. "Don't let them see you're scared."

"Good thing we're still coated with mud," Vicky muttered. "I think I peed myself."

* * *

The two Mrazors sped through the forest at a good clip for more than a mile until they reached an old footpath. Ving's Mrazor lurched to a stop and he shut the engine down.

"Well, that was fun," he said drily. Jared flicked the selector switch on his M-16 to "safe".

Vicky whirled around in the front seat to face Charlie.

"Headhunters?"

"No joke, Vicky. The Dayak are famous for their warlike culture and ferocity, and centuries ago they took the heads of their enemies and shrunk them. They believed the spirits of the heads they took would serve them in the afterlife. Shrinking the heads made them easier to transport."

"I thought headhunting was a thing of the past…"

"The Dayak went on a rampage about twenty years back. Groups of them, armed with spears, machetes and blowpipes, swept through the market town of Sampit in Central Kalimantan and killed more than two hundred Maduran refugees over a six-day period. The Dayak tribesmen swore to kill or drive out tens of thousands of migrant refugees from Madura Island because they were taking jobs and land. The bodies of their victims were scattered around in the streets of the town and the heads of many of the dead were taken as trophies by the tribesmen. Those 'machetes' we saw on their hips are not just for chopping through vegetation. The Dayak call them *"ambang"* and they are modeled after the *"mandau"*, which is the formal, or ceremonial, headhunter's sword."

Charlie grinned at the horrified look on Vicky's face. "For the most part the Dayak are peaceful hunter-gatherers these days, but deep in the interior there are pockets of Dayak who hold to the old ways."

Brad got out the map and his sat phone to check their position, cursed in a low voice and stepped off into the forest. Vicky hurried after him. She caught up to him just out of earshot of the rest of the team.

"What's wrong, Brad?" she asked quietly.

"Just mentally kicking myself, Vicky." He turned to face her. "I'm still alive because up until this mission I have been a consummate professional. I plan for everything; I have a backup plan for everything I can think of that might go wrong. I haven't been perfect, but I have been thorough." He turned away again. "This mission is different. I changed things around, I leaned on other people instead of double-checking everything myself, and as a result just about everything that could go wrong has gone wrong."

Vicky grabbed his shoulder and spun him back around so that they were face-to-face, and she was angry.

"Bullshit!" she hissed, her fists clenched in fury. "I'm not sure what's going on in that head of yours, but I know what I'm seeing with my own eyes and it's so out of character I'm having a hard time believing it! You've *always* had other people to depend on, people who've provided you with intel, people who've provided you with contacts you couldn't be a hundred percent sure of. You said it yourself; there's *never* been a mission where every little detail goes according to plan! One of your prime talents is your ability to assess the disasters and adapt to them decisively on the fly, but today you're acting like a brand new second lieutenant … second-guessing your every decision and trying to figure out why things have gone wrong. *Screw what's gone wrong!* You'd better get your head out of your ass and give us back the old Brad Jacobs or *none* of us is going to get out of this alive!" Vicky spun on her heel and stalked back to the rest of the team seething.

Brad's eyes dropped to the ground and his cheeks flushed with shame. Vicky had called it as she saw it ... and she was right. Accepting Ving as his business partner, trusting Willona's business acumen, using Charlie's Intel and his contacts ... none of it was really new. His team had formed around him because they trusted him, believed in him. He had lived his whole life by a code, a code that was not easy to live up to ... but it was his code, a Marine's code. He realized in that moment that he knew what had to be done and that he knew how to do it. In the final analysis, he would always be a Marine. A Recon Marine! His spine stiffened and his shoulders straightened. When he walked back to Team Dallas, he was walking tall.

"We've still got ten more miles to go before we reach Camp Bashir. We need to move faster if we're going to conduct a proper recon and then move at first light. I'll take the lead again, and we'll take trails and footpaths wherever possible." He turned to Vicky and handed her the sodden topographical map. "Try to follow the route we are taking on here. When you aren't sure where we are, tap me on the knee and I'll stop so we can verify by GPS."

He turned to Ving. "Stay as far back from me as you can, making sure you keep eye contact on the back of my Mrazor. We know now there are Dayaks in our A.O. (area of operations) that are armed with modern weapons as well as swords and blowguns. I don't want anybody taking us out all at once because we're bunched up. We spent sixty grand on these mechanical donkeys, and now their speed is going to justify their expense." He looked every member of the team in the face, one at a time. "Lock and load, weapons off safe!" he barked. "Saddle up and move! We have a hostage to rescue!"

* * *

It wasn't as if he didn't trust Amir Ibrahim to see to the proper execution of the live fire training. Ahmad Hamdani was a firm believer in the old adage that people did not tend to do what was expected of them but what their leaders *inspected*. It was for that reason that he climbed into his Jeep and left Camp Bashir for the training site, where he could lead his recruits by example, as was proper. Amir Ibrahim was not thrilled to relinquish control of the exercise, but he displayed no visible reaction to being relegated to leading a *regu*.

Hamdani poured the strong, sweet dregs of coffee from his canteen cup onto the coals of the small cookfire and then used a small amount of water from his canteen to rinse it out before wiping it dry with his bandana.

Restoring canteen and cup to its pouch on his belt, he looked over the line of *regu* until he found the teen Ibrahim had butt-stroked. The boy—he could not bring himself to refer to the teen as a man yet—was conscious and sitting up, rubbing the back of his head. Hamdani felt no rancor for Ibrahim's disciplining the recruit so harshly. Jemaah Islamiyah's works required training, discipline, and blind faith and the recruits had to learn absolute obedience to their instructions lest they fail the cause at a critical point. Losing a recruit or three in this phase of their training would be an inconvenience. Losing several or even a *regu* or two during the explosives training phase, or perhaps an experienced cadre member, would be an inexcusable waste of resources and training time.

"*Di kakimu!*" he bellowed. The recruits scrambled to their feet, hastily kicking at their small cook fires, stomping them out and pouring what was left of their coffee or tea on the coals. In seconds the fires were out, and the recruits were on line, weapons at their sides. None of them had even inserted a magazine. Hamdani's lesson had not been lost on them.

"Terapkan dalam garis skirmish!"

The instructors hurried to stand in front of their *regu* and then spread them out at the proper intervals in a skirmish line.

"Instruktur, ambil posmu!"

The instructors scurried to take their posts behind the *regu*. Hamdani was a hard taskmaster, and they knew he was as likely to discipline them as he was the recruits ... and he was about to order the recruits to lock and load their weapons. It was never wise to stand in front of an untrained village boy with a loaded rifle in his hands. Death in battle with the name of Allah on their lips was a guarantee of Paradise. Death in training at the hands of a village idiot was just a bad deal.

"Kunci dan muat senjata Anda!"

Thirty-five recruits tapped their magazines on their thighs to seat their rounds firmly and inserted them into the magazine wells of the M-16s until they heard the click that indicated it was locked in place. Then they gripped the forestocks of their weapons with their left hands and pulled their charging handles to the rear and released them, causing the top round in the magazines to load into the firing chambers. The exercise sounded rather like a class of high school students in a typing class, pecking away.

Hamdani's mouth curled into a moue of disgust and then he barked the order to move out.

"Pindah!"

Darkness was falling, and visibility was great. The moonlight was more than adequate for Hamdani to observe both the recruits and the instructors. There were no targets downrange; this was not to be an exercise in marksmanship. The purpose of the training was to teach the recruits to sustain a constant rate of suppressive fire over an objective, never allowing an opponent the opportunity to stick his head up and return fire. It was valuable training for conventional troops, but as far as Hamdani was concerned, it was an absolute waste of time and ammunition for the recruits of Jemaah Islamiyah.

He glanced down at his Swiss chronograph. It was dark, but he would give the recruits another hour of marching through the rainforest before ordering the live fire exercise to start. He needed to make certain the recruits did not get back to Camp Bashir until after daylight, and he needed to ensure that they were exhausted and ready for sleep.

Hadani's head lifted and he cocked it to one side, listening intently. He thought he had heard a faint buzzing in the distance, but he had lost it. *"Damned Dayak,"* he grumbled to himself. The local village had begun acquiring technology at an alarming rate about a year before, and they were getting bolder by the day. His scouts had advised him that several Dayak had been spotted bearing modern assault type rifles in their oil palm fields lately. If they had gotten bold enough to be running chainsaws or similar equipment in the rainforest at night, it might be time to teach them a lesson. The last thing he needed at the moment was a renegade group of natives running through the rainforest around Camp Bashir armed with modern weapons.

* * *

The speedometer was indicating forty miles per hour as Brad raced down the narrow double rut cart trail. The trees had closed in on both sides of the trail, and Charlie leaned forward to tap Brad's shoulder, motioning for him to pull over.

"This place looks awfully familiar, Brad. If I'm right, we should be about ten miles outside the camp right now."

"We can check that soon enough." Brad climbed out of the cockpit and motioned for Vicky to bring the map up to the hood. Charlie bent over to peer at the map as well as Vicky brought out a penlight with a red filter on it. She cupped her hand over the light and shone it on the map as Brad pulled up the GPS on his phone. Charlie looked at the digital readout on the phone and then peered down at the map. He grunted and put his index finger down on the now barely legible map.

"Yeah, this is it." He slid his finger forward a half inch or so. "Right here the rainforest opens up considerably. Second growth timber I guess… Whatever the reason, there's lighter undergrowth and the trees are a lot smaller. Everything's more spread out."

"Okay, take ten," Brad ordered. "Everybody stretch, get the kinks out, get yourselves some water, hit the head. We go from here to within about five klicks from the perimeter of the camp and I'll designate an O.R.P. (Objective Rallying Point) where we'll conceal the vehicles and set up a perimeter before conducting a recon to see exactly what we're facing." He didn't wait to see if there were any questions, he needed to hit the head rather badly himself.

Almost exactly ten minutes later, Team Dallas loaded up and set off down the trail at speed. Just at the point where the rainforest began to spread out, the night exploded with muzzle flashes and the sound of gunfire.

* * *

The buzzing noise had started up again shortly after he'd moved the recruits out on line. At first he was annoyed by the sheer audacity of the Dayak, and then he became angered. The buzzing sound grew louder and separated into the sound of two separate swarms of giant bees apparently coming up the cart trail to the right of his skirmish line. Overwhelmed by a great desire to annihilate the brash natives, Hamdani decided to intimidate them instead. Just as the two odd sounding and unexpectedly large, strange looking vehicles burst into view, Hamdani roared out the command to open fire.

"Buka api!"

The moonlight did not give him as good a look at the vehicles or the passengers as he needed, but he suspected he had misjudged the instant the recruits opened up. Hamdani screamed for a ceasefire as soon as the vehicles sped off the roadway and into the rainforest. He couldn't be certain, but the shadowy figures in the odd looking and sounding vehicles did not resemble any Dayaks he had ever seen.

He reached for his cell phone as he ran to the closest instructor to get him to call off the shooting. Unfortunately for him, for once the recruits seemed to insist on following their instructions to the letter, maintaining a constant rate of fire with no letup. It was several minutes before it was silent enough for Hamdani to call Camp Bashir.

* * *

Abdullah Darmadi, a brand new recruit, sat at a military style field desk beneath a tent fly erected outside the cottage of Ahmad Hamdani. The heat of the night and the buzz of the insects had made him sleepy, and he was having difficulty staying awake even after the dire warnings given him by the instructor who had assigned him night duty at lights out.

"You must stay awake at all times, and if anything unusual should happen, you must come to the cadre barracks and wake me up instantly, do you understand?"

"Yes *Tuan*," Abdullah had answered. He was newly arrived and very proud that the instructor had selected him to perform the important function of looking after the very important guest cleric

Hamdani as well as the grave responsibility of keeping the clipboard that the guards had to sign when they changed shifts. Abdullah himself had not yet learned to read or write, but the Imam in his village had promised that the leaders of Jemaah Islamiyah would teach him to do so.

The instructor had given him a cell phone, a technological marvel that Abdullah recognized but had never used, with his final instructions.

"This is the camp phone. Do not break it. Do not lose it. If someone should call, come immediately to the barracks and wake me up. Do you understand, boy?" Abdullah had nodded. "You must always answer an instructor, boy. A nod is not enough! Now, repeat your instructions back to me."

Abdullah had complied, pleased that he had remembered them word for word.

"I suppose that is good enough," the instructor said. "Now one more thing... *Tuan* Hamdani *is not to be disturbed for any reason!* Understand?"

"Yes *tuan.*"

The instructor, pleased with himself because he had pawned off his own boring guard detail on the unsuspecting recruit, hurried back to the cadre barracks for a night of blissful sleep beneath his mosquito netting. Abdullah waited until he was out of sight before picking up the cell phone and began to play with the buttons, some of which made the face light up as if by magic. One such button made strange writing appear on the face. Frightened that he might have damaged the marvel, he quickly set it back down on the desk and pretended he had never touched it. The light on the face displayed the words "Airplane Mode" for a period of time and then blinked out. Abdullah was relieved when the light went out.

SIXTEEN

The fusillade of rifle fire had scared the hell out of Brad and he had instinctively swerved off the road and into the relative safety of the rainforest.

"Ving is right behind us!" Vicky yelled.

Ving was following them, and Brad pushed on as fast as he was able, wanting to put as much distance between those guns and his team as fast as he could.

Zigging and zagging through the trees and around the thickest underbrush, he had been forced to turn on the headlights to avoid a collision. Until he had gone off-road at speed he had been able to see well enough by moonlight to drive. When he finally felt that it was safe to stop, he had absolutely no idea where he was in relation to Camp Bashir. He grabbed his M-16 from its carrier and climbed out of the Mrazor to wait for Ving to pull up behind him.

Vicky, Jessica, and Charlie were right behind him, weapons at the ready and facing outwards. Ving coasted to a stop mere seconds later, and he, Pete, and Jared were out in a flash.

"How the hell did they know we were coming?" Vicky asked.

"Jared says they weren't shooting at us," Pete said, "and I tend to agree with him."

"The only muzzle flashes I saw weren't pointed anywhere near us ... and it looked for all the world like a platoon live fire exercise, just like we had back in boot camp. Infantry in the assault."

"I just saw the muzzle flashes and heard the first volley," Brad mused, "but you're right, Jared, that's exactly what it resembled. But who in the hell would be practicing infantry tactics in the rainforest?"

"Charlie, can you think of a local militia or an insurgent group in this area, somebody trying to raise an army?" Jessica asked.

"I've never heard even a whisper of anything like that. There are several terrorist groups on the radar but no conventional militias. This doesn't make any sense at all."

"I'd like to know what that was all about myself, people, but right now we have to face the fact that *somebody* knows we're here … somebody with at least a platoon-sized force that is armed with modern weapons."

Every member of the team was privately mulling over this new development in a mission that was already out of whack. The odds, which had not been overwhelmingly in their favor from the start, were rapidly diminishing.

"Vicky, let me see that map again, please."

She pulled the map out, still wrapped in the cheap polyethylene poncho, and spread it out on the hood of the Mrazor. The smearing had gotten worse, but Charlie was familiar enough with the area that, with his help, Brad was able to orient himself.

"We have no way of knowing if that group is connected with JI at the camp or not. If they are, we have to assume they have some means of communicating with whoever is left behind."

"If they are connected, and if they have communications capabilities, Brad, we're screwed. They're going to know we're coming."

Brad gave Charlie a long questioning look.

"I don't like it, Brad, this is startin' to smell something awful."

"You think we should back up and regroup, Ving?"

"Either that or let's just go balls to the wall and go get Duckworth, Brad. If that was part of the group from the camp, they're gonna be understrength right now."

"If they don't beat us back to the camp," Jessica remarked.

Brad could sense the team's confidence bleeding away, and he knew instinctively that whatever he was going to do, he needed to do it quickly and decisively. He folded the sodden map with a crisp confidence that he didn't feel.

"We need to move quickly, 'balls to the wall' as you said, Ving. We're going to have to count on you, Charlie, to let me know when we're getting close, and we're going to have to leave a listening post near the main road to warn us if that group we just got away from comes back. That's a deviation from the original plan ... but that's the nature of the beast: improvise, adapt, overcome."

"What are we going to do if it goes sour, Brad?" Jessica, the least experienced member of the group, was the one who asked, but she had proven herself under fire before, and no one doubted her courage.

"If any one of you sees something that makes you believe the mission a no-go at any time, the code phrase for abort mission is 'longhorn cactus'."

Jared's snicker and comment gave them all a brief laugh.

"Nothin' like a little bit of Texas to make a feller feel secure."

It was just the note Brad wanted to end the briefing on.

"Saddle up, move out!"

* * *

It had taken them ten minutes of hard driving to get to the main road—a rough two-lane unimproved dirt road that didn't look like it had ever even had a nodding acquaintance with a road grader leading to what Charlie had told them was the front entrance to Camp Bashir. As far as Ving was concerned, Charlie had proved himself. It was his trust in his contacts from his former employment with the Department of State that was troubling.

Ving's experiences with the State Department and the C.I.A. had been sketchy over the years, and he had developed a deep mistrust of what he called the 'alphabet' agencies. The F.B.I., D.E.A., A.T.F., I.C.E. and all the others were far too prone to political intrigue and manipulation. Ving despised politics and politicians; he had seen their handiwork up close and personal in Afghanistan and Iraq, and to a lesser extent in most of the rest of the world.

He had been a little uncomfortable with Charlie's reliance on Daniel Novianti from the beginning. He had become a little more uneasy when Brad had so easily accepted the notion of depending on an arms dealer who was a complete unknown, and the unexpected presence of Waldingham at the meeting with Novianti on the beach had set off every alarm in Ving's head. The appearance of that black helicopter with that puke Waldingham hanging out the damned door had given him a leaden feeling in his gut that still hadn't gone away.

In all the years he had known Brad, the man had proved to be rock solid, the most dependable, trustworthy man Ving had ever known. His judgment had been better than Ving's own. This mission was the first time he had ever had any doubts about the man's abilities and, deep down inside, it hurt to admit to himself that he had. He had seen, though, the change in Brad at this last stop, and the cracks in his faith had begun to heal. Whatever doubts had been troubling the man, he seemed to have gotten a grip on them. Their situation had not improved, but having the old Brad back had bolstered Ving's confidence. The plan had changed, and they were aggressively pursuing a new plan. That was enough for Ving. He pushed down on the throttle harder. Brad's Mrazor was pulling away from him.

* * *

"Pull over here, Brad; if we go any closer they're going to hear us!" Charlie yelled. If his memory served him, they were about five or six klicks out from Camp Bashir.

Brad drove into a thicket of jungle ferns and shut down the Mrazor, and Ving followed. The whole team hurried to conceal the two ATVs from any but the closest scrutiny, both from the sides and the sky.

Brad glanced down at his chronometer.

"Best I can figure, we have about three hours before we have to be in position to execute whatever plan we come up with. We need to find and set up an O.R.P. and get our recon underway. Now listen … no shortcuts, got it? We do this right or we abort. I will not initiate this op with half-assed information or if we are so badly overmatched that we have no chance of success. We can't do Duckworth any good if we get ourselves killed trying to get him out." He stopped, looking each one of them directly in the eyes. "Everyone, now, check the batteries on your satellite phones."

There was a brief shuffling as phones were pulled out and battery statuses checked. One by one, they each responded with "Up."

"Good. Remember, the signal for abort is 'longhorn cactus'. Now, we're going to locate an easily recognizable site for an O.R.P. and then I'm going to send one of you back here to set up a listening post. Let's move."

Three minutes' walk brought them to a rise in the rainforest floor that held a giant Shorea tree rising high above its brothers. Near the top there was a white blaze that fairly glowed in the dark, the bark skinned off, apparently the result of a recent lightning strike. As if on cue, the rain started again. Brad stopped and raised his hand above his head, moving his fist in a circle to indicate that they were at the O.R.P.

"Vicky!" She looked up at him. "Set up an LP beside the road. Anything at all comes down that road call my phone as soon as they pass you." Vicky hurried off to assume her position without a backward glance.

Brad really wanted to participate in the recon himself, but he knew that Jared was more skilled at the task than he was and that Ving was almost as good ... and someone had to man the O.R.P.

Unfolding the sodden map once more, they verified their precise position with the GPS. Charlie pointed out the location of Camp Bashir once more, which was unnecessary as they had all pored over the map for hours. Brad slipped a clear, fluid filled compass suspended from a cord from around his neck and took an azimuth from the O.R.P. to the center of the camp.

Brad pointed a finger first at Jared then at Ving, and then he gave the signal that they had developed over the years for a three-hundred-sixty-degree recon. The two men took note of the azimuth and then faded into the rainforest.

Charlie, Jessica, Pete, and Brad spread out about twenty meters apart in a rough circle, taking cover as best they could while still maintaining visual contact with at least two of the others. They settled in for a long wait in the drizzling rain.

* * *

Jared loved a good ride a much as anyone, but the moment he embarked on the reconnaissance he felt like a wanderer who had returned home after a long journey. The rainforest welcomed him, enfolded him in its leafy embrace. He breathed deeply of the air, a combined scent of vegetation, moisture, earth, and decaying plants, leaves, and wood. It was as if he were being taken into the welcoming arms of an old lover.

Jared was a master sniper, and stealth was as necessary to his success as his extraordinary vision and his steady hands. He had become a living legend in Force Recon as much for his ability to become invisible as for his uncanny skills as a marksman. He became one with the rainforest, as much a part of it as the trees and plants. Even the small creatures that lived there were not disturbed by his passing as he crept towards Camp Bashir.

He smelled it before he saw it. The moment the smell of man assailed his nostrils, he froze, every one of his senses alive and seeking. Even with proper field sanitation techniques it was impossible to completely eradicate the odor of human waste, and the JI recruits disposed of theirs in the same manner U.S. troops had disposed of theirs in Vietnam a half century before, they mixed it with diesel fuel and burned it in steel drums. The odor was a distinctive one. The next smell that registered was that of the garlic they cooked with, followed rapidly by the fragrance of other spices … tamarind, chilies, pepper.

He didn't strain, he just relaxed and let his ears begin to pick up the surrounding sounds, and slowly he noticed that the man-made sounds began to separate themselves from the sounds of the jungle. First the metallic sounds … the clink of a metal sling keeper against wire, the click made by the sound of a Zippo lighter closing.

The sound of the lighter was closely followed by the unique fragrance of burning tobacco leaves.

Jared grunted. A sentry, thinking he was safely out of range of his supervisors, was sneaking a cigarette. Smokers seem to think that by cupping their hands over the glowing tip of their cigarettes they are concealing their activity, never realizing that a non-smoker can smell the aroma of burning tobacco—even the clove tobacco, called *kretek*, favored by Indonesians—from a considerable distance. An animal can smell if from even farther away. Jared wormed his way toward the source, the aroma growing stronger by the inch.

The sentry was little more than a boy, dressed in poorly dyed black cotton clothing. His M-16 was slung over his shoulder, and he was using both hands to cover the glow of the cherry-red tip of his *kretek*. His back was toward Jared, and it would only have taken a single bound to reach him. It would have been a simple task to put one hand over his mouth to keep him silent and use his free hand to insert his boot knife beneath the boy's sternum, angling the tip upward into his heart.

Jared had done that more times than he cared to think about.

Throat slitting, like they did in the movies, was a stupid way to take out someone if silence was necessary, people made a god-awful amount of noise when they suddenly grew another mouth beneath their chin. The Corps taught a method whereby an opponent was taken from behind and dispatched with a swift wrench of the head and subsequent breaking of the neck, but even that could be too loud in the relative silence of the rainforest.

The problem was that Jared didn't want to take the chance of alerting the other sentries or the supervisors, especially since he had no idea how many there were and what their disposition was. All he could really do was back away from the sentry and continue with his reconnaissance. Any other action he took could jeopardize the mission. He began to back away, a fraction of an inch at a time, while the boy sentry smoked, unconcerned, and stared at the moonbeams beginning to peek through the broken cloud cover. The rain had diminished considerably, thinning out to a light drizzle. The drops falling off the trees were larger and louder than the ones falling from the sky.

* * *

Ving moved through the rainforest as silently as a wraith, surprisingly fluid and graceful for a man of his bulk. Where Jared stayed low and utilized ground cover for concealment, Ving relied on light and shadow, taking advantage of trees and their shadows to break his image into irregular shapes not easily recognizable by the human eye, combined with a remarkable ability to become perfectly still. Instructors over the years had referred to the technique as "situational camouflage," and it worked in any environment, from desert to jungle to the Arctic Circle. As far as Ving was concerned, they could call it whatever they wanted ... all he cared about was that it had worked reliably for him on several continents.

Ving had paced off about four klicks when he noticed the sentry. He froze, half in the shadows cast by the tangled roots of a young Shorea. The roots resembled the root system of mangrove trees though far larger. The sentry turned suddenly, staring right at the spot where Ving was standing. Motionless, holding his breath, Ving fought off the urge to swallow the huge lump of fear lodged in his throat. The trigger finger on the hand wrapped around the pistol grip of his M-16 itched, his survival instincts in overdrive. The sentry, uncertain, hesitated for what seemed an eternity. Then, amazingly, he turned away to stare back in the direction of the camp. The sentry glanced warily around the camp, carefully slipped his M-16 off his shoulder and concealed it under a rotten log. Then he skulked away into the rainforest.

What the hell? Ving wondered. *Deserter?* It had never occurred to him before that fanatic organizations like JI might have problems with deserters, but he could come up with no other explanation for the sentry's behavior. A frown creased his broad, dark face. A deserter was a loose end, and there were already too many loose ends on this mission. A deserter wandering around in the area was a variable there was no way to control, and that was a risk the team couldn't afford. There was no telling which way the sentry would swing if he encountered the team.

Ving followed the deserter who was slinking along a footpath that skirted the camp, apparently a path worn by the roving sentries on their rounds. The man stuck to the path for a very short distance before coming to a full stop and looking nervously back over his shoulder towards the camp. Ving, frozen mid-stride, heart pounding, held his breath once more, readying himself mentally for an all-out rush for the sentry should he turn back and see his stalker. Instead, the sentry took a deep breath and scurried into the rainforest, away from the camp.

Ving knew he had to make a decision, and he did so without hesitating any longer. In absolute silence, he closed the distance between himself and the deserter, clapping one immense hand over the deserter's mouth and manhandling him to the ground. The deserter struggled wildly when Ving closed off his nose as well, but his struggles subsided and then ceased as he lost consciousness. Ving quickly tore strips from the man's rough cotton shirt, doubling them for added strength before tying his hands behind his back. Another strip bound the deserter's ankles, and Ving used the rope belt the deserter wore to tie the strips together, effectively hog-tying the hapless man. Ving used his own bandana to gag his captive.

Great move, Ving, now what the hell are you going to do with this bozo? You can't just leave him out here to die … he may be a damned terrorist in training, but he was leaving. Gotta give him credit for that. You can't carry him on this recon, that's for damned sure.

He scanned the trail behind him and selected a massive Shorea tree; then he hoisted the deserter over his shoulder and took him to the root base, stashing him on the side away from the path and covering him with branches and leaves. Standing back, he scrutinized his handiwork and decided that it would do in the semi-darkness. He stepped around to the path side of the tree and used his combat knife to cut a blaze in the bark to mark the spot so that he could recognize it on the way back to the O.R.P.

Unwilling to take any more time away from his recon, Ving hurried to get a better look at the camp.

* * *

Vicky huddled under a sort of tunnel formed by the broad fronds of a palmetto plant, her view of the rough, unpaved road clear for a considerable distance. The moon was peeking through a break in the cloud cover, casting a dim glow over the roadway so that the wisps of fog emanating from the forest floor looked ghostly.

Perfect locale for a horror movie set, she thought absently. She shivered despite the heat and mugginess, acutely aware of the extreme sketchiness of the mission. She had seen the doubt on Brad's face ... just as she had seen his determination beat the doubt back. There was no question in her mind that he had recovered from whatever had thrown him, but she was also aware that there were several planning issues left that needed to be resolved, and she wondered briefly if her growing love for the man had clouded her own judgment. She dismissed the thought as quickly as it had slipped into her mind. Brad's judgment and his acumen had impressed her from the first time she had met him, at the resort in Acapulco. She knew him well enough now to know that whatever had been distracting him had been shunted aside or resolved. Brad was back, he had been decisive and fully in command again when he had sent her to establish a listening post and selected Jared and Ving for the recon.

She settled in to wait for the signal to come back to the O.R.P. The wait seemed interminable; the only activity around her was that of the monkeys cavorting in the trees around her and the frantic movements of the ants she had disturbed when she lay down across their work trail.

* * *

Ahmad Hamdani had been disconcerted by the unexpected appearance of the two ATVs as well as by the lack of discipline and confusion in his recruits. Despite the best efforts of his cadre, it had taken several minutes to get the recruits under control. Some of them had turned and fired at the

ATVs, and one had even turned and fired some rounds back in Hamdani's general direction. It had taken every ounce of Hamdani's self-control to keep him from terminating that particular recruit. He had finally called a halt and set the recruits to making coffee or tea for themselves again while he conferred with his cadre members regarding the bewildering appearance of the ATVs.

None of them had seen anything quite like those particular ATVs before, nor had they ever heard any so quiet. The INP had nothing like them, and the JI's deep-cover asset inside the *Gegana* had not mentioned anything about them either. The consensus of the cadre members was that, since the intruders hadn't fired on them, it was most likely that they were poachers and, therefore, no threat. It was nearly three a.m. before the discussion ended, and the recruits were getting drowsy. Hamdani remained unconvinced, though he allowed himself to be persuaded to restart the live fire drill against his better judgment.

Ten minutes into the exercise, unable to escape a nagging premonition in the back of his head, he turned the exercise over to his senior instructor and stalked over to the perfectly maintained military surplus Jeep that he had driven to the site of the exercise and turned it towards Camp Bashir. The closer he got to the camp the stronger and more persistent the premonition became. He pressed on the accelerator, pushing the Jeep harder than he should have on the rough, unpaved road.

* * *

Vicky, startled, looked up from her study of the busy ants when she heard the sound of a gasoline engine approaching fast. She saw the headlights sweeping around a bend in the road about two hundred meters back just as she began to hear the rattle and clank of suspension parts negotiating the ruts and potholes in the road. She barely had time to pull up Brad's number and key the handset before the Jeep swept past her at a reckless pace. Brad didn't even acknowledge the call, he just listened.

"Incoming. One vehicle, one driver. Out!" She settled back down, on wide alert, to wait for Brad's summons to return to the O.R.P. It wouldn't be long, she could feel it.

* * *

Brad stared at the sat phone in his hand as he punched in the numbers for Jared and Ving. He sent the recall signal that would trigger their sat phones, light and vibration only. The signal light on the phones was simply a tiny sliver of plastic that glowed a low intensity red, barely noticeable from more than a couple of feet away.

* * *

Jared felt rather than saw the sat phone signal to return at the same time as he heard the sound of a Jeep approaching. His natural and professional curiosity caused him to hesitate long enough to observe the Jeep speed through the main gate to the camp and skid to a stop in front of the smallest of the three permanent buildings inside the perimeter of the camp.

The man who climbed out of the Jeep was tough looking, a hard-bitten Middle Eastern type with hawkish features, and he looked agitated. The man climbed down out of the Jeep and stormed into the concrete block house and closed the door behind him. Jared puzzled over the man's behavior for a moment and then slipped away, like a ghost in the forest.

* * *

"What are we going to do with him, Brad?" Pete asked, jerking his thumb at the trussed-up sentry that Ving had carried into the O.R.P. over his shoulder like a sack of cattle feed.

"I don't know yet. Terrorist or not, he's just a kid."

"A kid that would have been happy to blow us to hell when we got into that camp," Pete groused.

"He was deserting," Ving said shortly. "I wasn't going to take out a kid who was deserting... I won't kill him."

Brad eyed his best friend evenly. In principle, he agreed with Ving, but the kid was going to be a real complication. It didn't matter; he would deal with the problem. Improvise, adapt, overcome.

"Sand table!" he ordered, dismissing the captive for the moment.

Ving and Jared sank to the ground in a clear, flat spot and began to scrape aside the leaves and vegetation. When they had an area of bare dirt, they began to speak in turn, using twigs, symbols, and vegetation to create what was in effect a scale model, like a diorama, of Camp Bashir and its occupants.

"Sentries posted on the perimeter, here, here, and here," Ving said, pointing out the locations around the outside of the camp. "This one"—he pointed at the recumbent form of the captive who was apparently frozen with fear—"I took down right here." He indicated the final spot he had pointed out. "They're young, they're inexperienced, and evidently they're not being supervised ... at least, I never spotted a sergeant of the guard."

"Me neither," said Jared. "I only spotted two sentries, here and here. They don't seem to be moving much in the dark, they're not roving and don't seem to be making contact with each other. There's another guy here," he continued, pointing at a square he had drawn in the dirt. "He's sitting under a tent fly in front of this building, which looks like a jail. It has a steel door, and, unlike the other two buildings, it doesn't seem to have any windows. This slightly larger building here looks like it might be where the cadre sleeps. This smallest building is set apart from the other two, so I'm guessing the camp commander stays there; that Jeep driver that came in went straight inside the smaller building."

"Troop tents are over here," Ving said. "Lined up but not with string, the way we did it in boot camp. Looks like about thirty or forty troops billeted down there, but the weird thing is I didn't see any movement in the camp at all until that Jeep came roaring in. If that guy was the commander, he sure as hell didn't notice the guy under the tent fly scrambling to his feet. That guy was sound asleep before the Jeep came through the gate."

"He won't be sleeping now." Brad turned to Jared. "You say he just barged right on inside the little building?"

"Didn't even knock."

"And, Ving, you didn't see any other movement at all?"

"Nope, like I said, it was weird. With that many people, you'd expect to see *somebody* moving. Making a piss call, sneaking a smoke, something…"

Brad studied the sand table for several long moments.

"Are you guys thinking what I'm thinking?"

"Those guys we ran into are the JI out on a training exercise?" Jared asked.

"Makes sense," Ving agreed. "That would explain the lack of activity and the rookies on sentry duty."

"That also means those shooters could be on their way back by now. I wish we'd had time to check them out. We have no way of knowing if they have transport or not. We're going to have to do a snatch and grab, in and out before those guys get back or anybody left in camp can react."

"We're going to have to leave a listening post out on the road too," Jared said soberly. "Vicky's going to be pissed if you leave her out of your 'lightning strike'."

Brad grunted unhappily. "Vicky's a trooper. She won't like it, but she'll understand."

"If you say so," Ving said, chuckling. "Glad I don't have to tell her."

"We have bigger problems, Ving. Like you said, Jared, this has to be a lightning strike, so we have to figure out a way to take down that door quick, fast, and in a hurry."

"Ving, go replace Vicky at the LP for a few minutes, I want to get her take on this and see if she has any ideas." Brad called out in a stage whisper, telling Jessica, Charlie, and Pete to come over to the sand table. They kneeled around the sand table expectantly.

"I don't want to do this twice. Vicky will be here any minute now," Brad said. All of them studied the sand table until Vicky came rushing up at a jog.

"What's up?" she asked.

Brad gave a brief summary of Jared and Ving's recon and identified the buildings in the camp.

"What we have to figure out is how to get in there, take down the steel door, grab Duckworth, and get out before anybody can react or those troops get back here. If I'm right about those shooters, we've got to get moving and soon."

Vicky took in the sand table and frowned in concentration. Then her brow smoothed out and she smiled.

"Anybody know how to hot-wire a Jeep?" she asked brightly.

* * *

"Don't take it so hard, Brad, I know somebody has to keep an eye out for those guys. Rookies or not, they have guns and they aren't going to be happy about us spoiling their hostage scenario. They're young, but they will kill you without a qualm."

Brad had taken her out of earshot of the others because he hadn't wanted the others to see her reaction to being left out of the fireworks. She had surprised him. Vicky had wrapped her arms around his neck and kissed him deeply.

"Take care, Brad. I want you back." She turned and hurried back to her LP.

SEVENTEEN

"Ready?" Brad asked. Everyone responded with the thumbs up sign. He raised his hand, waved it in a circle, and pointed forward. Both Mrazors coughed into life and began to move through the rainforest toward the road.

Vicky watched silently, not giving away her position even to her team as the Mrazors sped off toward the camp. She clamped her jaws down in grim determination, flipped the selector switch on her M-16 to full auto, and then lined up three magazines on the ground in front of her. If the shooters came, they would have to get through her first. She had two more magazines in the cargo pockets of her trousers, and they would stay there. If she was forced to engage the JI shooters, she would empty as many of the magazines in front of her as she could and then flee into the rainforest. The others might see her as a lookout, but Vicky Chance was a warrior. She would not only provide her team with a warning, she would give them a more precious gift. She would give them time.

* * *

The Mrazors were running wide open, perhaps sixty miles per hour. Brad, who had relinquished the steering wheel, was sitting in the right front seat, his weapon on full auto. One foot rested on the outer rail of the frame and he was leaning precariously out the side. Charlie was in the driver's seat, hunched over the wheel, his heart racing.

Jessica sat in the back seat, mentally reviewing what she knew about the ignition system of her own Jeep, a restored CJ-7 that had been a gift from her father, Jack Paul, a wealthy international businessman who happened to be Brad's uncle. She had volunteered immediately when Jared had described the Jeep driven by the man they believed to be the camp commander. Jessica did all the work on her own Jeep, preferring to perform all maintenance and repairs herself. It would be up to her to start and drive the commander's Jeep.

Jared, Ving and Pete followed close behind in the second Mrazor. Ving and Pete held their weapons at the ready. They were racing towards a Jemaah Islamiyah training camp with only speculation and a short observation for preparation. If they were lucky, the odds might be slightly in their favor. If they were not lucky, the mission could become a fiasco. All of them were worried but not afraid. Brad Jacobs was a leader of men, and they knew it better than anyone. They had been under the gun before, all of them, and it had been with Brad, a Marine's Marine. They would have followed him into Hell, and each of them prayed silently to the gods of war that they were not doing precisely that.

* * *

Amir Ibrahim signaled for the other cadre members to call for a ceasefire, which really wasn't hard to do because the recruits were running low on ammunition. He squinted at the face of his watch and noted that there was precious little time before dawn. It was time to march the recruits to the truck and make their way back to Camp Bashir. The excitement of the night and Hamdani's abrupt departure had thrown the recruits way off their schedule.

The truck, an old Mitsubishi Fuso Fighter ton and a half stake body, was concealed in a draw half a mile through the rainforest to the rear of the training area. Ibrahim was not about to have to go to his superiors to ask for another truck just because Hamdani had insisted on sending the troops out with live ammunition before they were properly trained. He understood Hamdani's concerns for Duckworth's life, but his personal opinion had been that it would be far wiser to beef up the security around the camp rather than send the recruits away.

Hamdani was an acknowledged explosives expert, but as far as Ibrahim was concerned, the man was an unknown quantity as a "boots on the ground" fighter and that was the purpose of this class of recruits. Jemaah Islamiyah was preparing a hard push into the cities, and it would require the recruits to have a working knowledge of I.E.D.s (Improvised Explosive Devices), but their main purpose would be to master the intricate skills of heavy, house-to-house urban fighting. Ibrahim himself should have remained in charge of Camp Bashir.

Ibrahim stood between two of the cadre instructors, who were holding rough burlap bags to collect the recruits' magazines. As each recruit prepared to climb onto the bed of the truck, Ibrahim personally inspected each weapon's firing chamber to ensure that it was empty. He was willing to give his life in battle with the name of Allah on his lips, but he was not willing to die because an untrained recruit accidentally discharged his weapon during transport.

When the recruits were all packed aboard the stake body truck, Ibrahim waved one of the instructors into the cab, along with the burlap bags full of magazines. Then he and the other cadre instructors climbed into an old U.S. Army jeep that had somehow managed to survive the Vietnam War before being transported by oceangoing barge to Kalimantan along with a parcel of heavy equipment abandoned by the U.S. when they had withdrawn in defeat from South Vietnam in 1975. Jemaah Islamiyah had gotten an unbelievable treasure trove of weapons and equipment because of the stupendous wastefulness of American politicians, and they had made good use of it.

He tried to call Hamdani on his satellite phone, but the arrogant prick seemed to have turned it off. Ibrahim had impatiently disconnected the call and punched in the number for the phone he had left with Abdullah. No answer. Cursing, Ibrahim angrily punched the "power" button on his own phone and stuffed it into his shirt pocket.

"Kembali ke kamp!" (Back to the camp) he growled to his second-in-command, who promptly cranked up the jeep and turned around to lead the truck back to the main road.

* * *

Charlie was hard pressed to keep the Mrazor on the rough surface as he bore down on the last curve before the straightway that led to the gate of Camp Bashir. Unless the gate guard was sound asleep, he was going to know that the diesel engine sounds did not belong to friendlies, and he would be on the alert. He would have to depend on Brad and Jessica to take the man out before he could fire on the Mrazor. He grimly gripped the wheel harder, flipped his headlights on bright, and tried to coax a little more speed out of the turbo diesel engine.

The gate guard still had his M-16 leaning against the gate post when he heard the odd sounding engines, and he strained to get a glimpse of whatever was coming at him. The turbo diesel engines were quieter than one might expect, and the sudden appearance of brilliant headlights blinded him for a second. By the time he had blinked his eyes enough times to regain his vision, the Mrazors were on him. A crazy looking white man was leaning out the far side of the ATV, pointing a rifle at him, and a golden-haired woman was leaning out the near side. He grabbed his own rifle and tried to aim it just as he saw the muzzle flashes and felt the bullets rip into his midsection. He never heard the rifle go off.

Charlie manhandled the Mrazor over the ruts just inside the gate, aiming directly for the smaller cinder block building with the Jeep parked at an angle in front of it. He didn't let the ruts slow him down. As soon as he got close to the Jeep, he put the Mrazor into a sideward skid, bleeding off speed as he brought it to a halt behind the Jeep. Jessica leaped out before the ATV had come to a full halt and raced for the driver's seat of the Jeep. Brad was right behind her.

Ving swung his Mrazor out to the left side of Charlie's and steered for the windowless cinder block building where he was sure Duckworth was being held. Ignoring the shower of mud from Charlie's wheels, Ving skidded to a halt and jumped out from behind the wheel, rushing to the steel door. He heard Pete's M-16 chattering behind him and saw the JI recruit sprawled out on the ground beneath the tent fly, a satellite phone still in his hand. An M-16 stood untouched, leaning against the cinder block wall.

"Duckworth!" Ving shouted, pounding on the steel door with his big fist. "Duckworth! Can you hear me?"

Jared and Pete had rushed over to the gap between the cinder block buildings, keeping a lookout for hostiles coming from the tent area or the larger building. Several men tugging on black cotton clothing and carrying rifles poured out of the larger building, and Jared and Pete together mowed them down in three to six-round bursts. The two team members spread apart and advanced on the block building, keeping an eye on the row of recruit tents.

"Duckworth!" Ving screamed again, still pounding on the heavy steel door.

When Duckworth answered, he did so hesitantly.

"What do you want?" he asked weakly, afraid that his captors were tormenting him.

"We're Americans, Duckworth! We're here to take you home!"

Jessica dumped her M-16 in the floorboard of the Jeep and dove underneath the steering column. She slipped a penlight from her shirt pocket into her mouth and twisted it on then reached for the wires to the starter switch. Ripping three wires loose, she quickly stripped the insulation back from all three ends using her fingernails and then twisted the two ignition wires together. She checked to see that the gearshift was in neutral and then touched the hot wire to the ignition wires.

Brad glanced over at her when he heard the sound of the engine turning over, and the momentary distraction nearly got him killed.

* * *

Ahmad Hamdani heard the unfamiliar sound of the turbo diesels as they raced through the front gate. The sound of shots being fired galvanized him, and he didn't bother putting on his shirt. He grabbed his rifle and stuffed his feet into his wet boots without lacing them and sprinted out the door of his quarters.

A tall, muscular blond man with a short haircut stood straddle-legged beside the Jeep, M-16 at the ready. He was staring at a sight Hamdani had never expected to see at Camp Bashir, a pretty blonde woman sitting behind the steering wheel of the Jeep. The blond man swung around when Hamdani burst out the screen door of his quarters and leveled his rifle. Just as the muzzle of the rifle flared, Hamdani's feet tangled in the loose laces of his boot and he tumbled to the ground in front of the white man, his rifle skittering ahead of him, coming to rest beneath the Jeep.

"Shit!" the man swore out loud.

As the man brought his weapon down to bear on his body, Hamdani lunged at the bigger man's knees, taking him down to the mud and crawling atop him. Desperate, Hamdani scrabbled for the *karambit* he carried in a leather holster in the small of his back. As he got a grip on the handle, the white man hit him beneath the chin, sending him sprawling in the mud.

The white man was quick as a snake, lunging on top of Hamdani as soon as his back hit the mud. Blindly, Hamdani struck out with the razor sharp curved blade of the *karambit*, feeling it sinking into the flesh of the white man. He heard the man's gasp of pain and felt the hot gush of blood spilling over his fingers just as the man's elbow struck his chin. Everything went black.

* * *

Brad heard the gunshots and the sound of Jessica grinding the gears on the Jeep as she guided it to the building where Ving was pounding on the door with his fist. As he leaped on top of the terrorist, he felt a searing pain in his side, just below his ribcage. Ignoring the intense pain, he raised his arm and brought his elbow down on the man's chin as hard as he could. There was a satisfying crunch and then the man went limp beneath him.

Brad rolled off the half-naked man and clapped his hand over the gaping cut in his side. Gingerly, he explored the cut, tracing the outline of it with his forefinger. His whole hand came back covered in blood. The wound was bad, but he thought he could stanch the bleeding with his own damp, sweaty tee shirt until he could get somewhere to bind it properly. He grimaced. The rainforest was no place to go wandering around with an open cut, but he had a mission to finish and he would prefer to do that alive.

He turned the terrorist over and the man flopped like a rag doll, and Brad stripped off the man's boots, using the long laces to bind his hands and feet tightly. Then Brad peeled off his own shirt and tee shirt. As he lifted his tee shirt over his head, he heard the Jeep impact the steel door of the building Ving was standing in front of.

Jessica looked over her shoulder at the door she had just clobbered with the back of the Jeep and saw that it was hanging crazily from its hinges. Ving waved her away, and she moved forward a couple of feet. Ving planted one of his size fifteen boots square in the middle of the door and it crashed to the concrete floor inside the block building.

"Jared!" Ving roared as he raced inside the building.

* * *

Duckworth cowered in the corner of the room, afraid to look up because he was afraid that it was a trick designed to torment him. When he felt an immense pair of hands grab his shoulders and lift him from the floor as easily as his own wife might have lifted her damned little Chihuahua, he looked up into the grinning visage of the biggest, blackest sonofabitch he had ever seen.

"Ving's Taxi Service," the grinning monster said. "You lookin' for a ride home, brother?"

At that moment a tall, rangy man with a smoking M-16 in his hands stepped through the hole where the steel door had been just moments before.

"You gonna stay in here an' play patty cake or you wanna get outta this hellhole?" Jared drawled.

Duckworth recognized a Texas accent when he heard one, and he felt a rush of relief that was palpable.

"Thank God," he croaked. "I thought I was going to die here." Emotion overwhelmed him and he passed out in Ving's arms.

* * *

Brad was trying to drag Hamdani to the Mrazor when Jessica reached him.

"Brad, you're hurt!" she exclaimed.

He managed a weak grin.

"No kidding!" He grunted with pain. "Help me get this sonofabitch in the Mrazor. If he doesn't die from me bustin' him in the mouth he might have some information that will get that asshole Waldingham off our backs."

Jessica didn't hesitate. She grabbed one of Hamdani's legs and tugged at him. Together they wrestled the unconscious man into the back seat of the Mrazor and Charlie strapped him in as Brad staggered into the front seat.

Jared and Ving ran out of the building carrying the still handcuffed Duckworth between them.

Pete jumped into the other Mrazor, which Ving already had cranked.

"Go! Go! Go!" he yelled. The two Mrazors sped toward the front gate, the sound of shouts and sporadic gunfire behind them.

* * *

Vicky heard the sound of the Mrazors racing toward her, and she quickly scooped up the magazines she had laid out before her, stuffing them inside her shirt. When the two ATVs slewed to a complete stop in front of her, she dove into the second seat without even glancing at the passengers.

"I'm in!" she yelled. "Go!" The Mrazors raced off before she could even sit up straight. Bouncing around in the skittering vehicle, she fumbled for and found the seat belts and managed to strap herself in. It was only then that she noticed that Brad was slumped over in the front seat.

"Jesus Brad!" she yelled.

"He's hurt ... bad I think," Jessica said, just over the muted roar of the turbo diesels.

Vicky tried to unbuckle her seat belt so that she could get to him, but Charlie stayed her hands.

"There's nothing you can do until we get far enough away to stop," Charlie said. "He used his tee shirt to stop the bleeding, and it seems to be working so far."

Vicky glared at Charlie, but she knew he was right. Breaking the tee shirt loose from the wound would more than likely cause him to bleed freely again, and, judging from the amount of blood soaking the tee shirt, might cause him to bleed out. She had to cross her fingers and hope that they could reach someplace they could stop ... and soon.

* * *

Rafi Kusuma crawled out of his tent as soon as the shooting stopped and the sound of the engines faded in the distance. Carefully, he peered around the cadre building and then around the front of Hamdani's quarters. He saw Abdullah's body at the same time he noticed the missing door on the cinder block building where the hostage had been held. He had seen dead bodies before but not one belonging to someone he had shared a meal with just hours before. The sight made him sick to his stomach, and he was afraid he might spew.

Only then did the significance of the missing door and the bashed in Jeep hit him. The thought of Amir Ibrahim's reaction turned his fear into a reality, and he promptly bent over at the waist and hurled.

Wiping his mouth with the back of his hand, he walked slowly over to Abdullah's body and lifted the satellite phone gingerly from the dead sentry's grip. With shaking hands, he powered up the phone and punched in the number for Ibrahim's phone.

When Ibrahim answered on the second ring, Rafi lost it.

"*Tuan!* He's gone! They took him!"

* * *

Amir Ibrahim slammed the satellite phone down in his lap and cursed colorfully. When he was through, he ordered his driver to increase his speed. The recruit on the phone, Rafi Kusuma, had revealed that Duckworth had been taken by persons unknown. That in itself was not particularly surprising, Duckworth was a man of great influence in both finance and politics, which was one of the reasons Jemaah Islamiyah had targeted him. There was another reason as well, but Fadlhan had not seen fit to reveal it to him. The most interesting revelation Kusuma had made was that Hamdani was missing as well, which posed some rather interesting questions.

Ibrahim shook his head as if to clear it. Help was nearby; he knew exactly what he had to do. Picking up the satellite phone, he dialed a number so secret that he had committed it to memory rather than store it in the phone.

EIGHTEEN

The Mrazors were capable of speeds of more than sixty miles per hour, and Jessica and Ving were pushing them dangerously close to their limits. Brad was not talking, fighting the pain, so Jessica was following the last strategy she had heard discussed, sticking to the main road leading back to Sebamban and trusting to the unusual speed capabilities of the Mrazors to get them safely out of reach of the JI troops. Dawn was approaching with alarming speed, so she switched off the headlights.

In the backseat of Ving's Mrazor, Duckworth was a mess. Bruised, battered, and brain fogged from the isolation, sensory deprivation, and his refusal to eat the slop his captors had tried to feed him, he was struggling to understand why he was still handcuffed after he had been rescued. Jared, trying hard to reassure the oil magnate, was busy trying to pick the locks on the handcuffs, but the ride was far too rough for him to have much success.

Every bump and jolt sent bolts of pain flashing through Brad's body. He turned his mind inward, seeking his center, forcing himself to think of pleasant, peaceful things instead of the blinding pain in his side. He inhaled deeply through his nose until his lungs filled to bursting and then exhaled through his mouth until his lungs were empty, then he repeated the simple breathing exercise. Gradually the pain became muted, still present but isolated in a compartment within his mind. It was a technique he had used successfully before, and, mercifully, it worked once more. He straightened up in the seat and was relieved to find that the pain remained manageable in its compartment. Still doing his breathing exercises, he twisted in his seat to check his range of motion. Swiveling to his left was less painful than swiveling to his right, and the turn to his right caused the blood to well up and soak his tee shirt.

He felt a tap on his shoulder and saw a tee shirt drop across his shoulder, a woman's tee shirt. Despite the pain, he grinned at the thought of Vicky sitting on the back seat in her bra and jeans, knowing that she would be shrugging back into her faded chambray work shirt while Charlie was getting an eyeful. A second later, he got another surprise, this time from Charlie. A section of three-inch yellow nylon from the end of a cargo strap that had been used to tie the Mrazors down in the aircraft was draped over his shoulder, and he knew instinctively why it had been given to him.

Brad pressed Vicky's tee shirt down over his own bloody one and then used the wide strap to bind the shirts tightly to his body. The pressure hurt at first, but the strap pulled the smooth edges of the cut together and helped stop the fresh bleeding. The pain became manageable, and he took note of their surroundings as the vehicles raced toward Sebamban.

Charlie had been confused, and embarrassingly aroused, when Vicky had suddenly shucked off her faded chambray shirt and stripped off her tee shirt. Vicky did not have large breasts, but they were extremely shapely and the sports bra she wore beneath the tee shirt did little to conceal them. The redhead was an extraordinarily good looking woman and a bit of an exhibitionist. Understanding had dawned on him when she leaned forward to give the tee shirt to Brad. He instantly thought of taking off his belt to help bind the shirt to Brad's waist and had already started to do so when another thought, a memory, burst into his mind. The yellow nylon cargo straps that had been used to tie the Mrazors to the pallets for air shipment had been rolled up and placed in a compartment under the seats. The three-inch-wide straps would provide much better support for the makeshift bandage than his much narrower leather belt would.

He fumbled beneath the seat and removed one of the straps. Using his combat knife, he cut off a five-foot length of the yellow strap and laid it across Brad's shoulder. Then he sat back and averted his eyes as Vicky put her shirt back on—and he saw it.

The black helicopter was flying at treetop level and he could clearly see Waldingham flapping his hand at the door gunner and then at the Mrazors. The door gunner swiveled his pedestal mounted machine gun and pointed…

"Get off the road!" he screamed, thumping Jessica on the back with his left hand. At that moment the gunner fired, and rounds started kicking up mud in front of the speeding Mrazors. Charlie raised his M-16 and started firing wildly at the chopper. The chopper jockey jerked back on the stick and the bird climbed steeply in evasive action.

Jessica jerked her steering wheel hard to the left, sending the Mrazor off the road full tilt, braking hard and valiantly battling the crazily bucking vehicle to keep it from slamming into the giant tree trunks. Brad, grunting with pain, was trying to fire his M-16 one-handed at the chopper.

Jared had looked up from trying to pick Duckworth's handcuffs as soon as he'd heard Charlie's M-16 open up, and Pete started firing then. Ving, seeing Jessica swerve hard to the left and Charlie shooting upward, slammed his Mrazor hard in the other direction, to the right and into the rainforest. He switched off his engine as soon as he came to a halt beneath the thick canopy formed by giant hardwoods.

"Jesus!" he bellowed. "Get him out of this thing and under cover!" He grabbed his rifle from its scabbard and dove for cover.

"I never even heard it," Jessica groaned. The sudden silence, broken only by the sound of the helicopter rotor far above them, made her groan sound like a scream.

"What the hell's he doing?" Charlie muttered, trying to peer through the thick overhead canopy.

"He's bird-dogging," Brad said through clenched teeth. "Ving!" he shouted.

"We're good," Ving called out from across the road.

"Duckworth?"

"Nobody's hit, Brad, we're all good!"

"He's bird-dogging!"

"Shit!"

"What does that mean, 'bird-dogging'?" Jessica asked.

"It means he's spotting for somebody," Vicky said grimly.

"He has somebody on the ground?" Jessica queried, horrified at the prospect. As if on cue, they all heard the sound of vehicle motors approaching.

"Keep that chopper jockey busy!" Jared called out, low crawling toward the edge of the roadway. "I got this!"

Ving stared after the gangly sniper.

"I got your back, brother," he called out and dove for the ground, ready to crawl after Jared.

"Musa Qala!" Jared called back over his shoulder. "Keep the chopper occupied, dammit!"

"You almost got your dumb ass greased at Musa Qala!" Ving retorted, but he found cover and began to take aimed shots at the soaring helicopter.

"Musa Qala?" Jessica asked, peering through the canopy above and firing single shots whenever she caught a glimpse of the helicopter through the leaves and branches.

"Ask him later," Brad muttered. The pain was back, and it was intense. It took every ounce of self-discipline he possessed to concentrate on shooting at the helicopter. Whoever the chopper jockey was, he was one hell of a pilot. The Huey was bouncing around in the sky like a rabid squirrel in a cage.

Musa Qala was a village in Helmand Province, Afghanistan, and Jared had single-handedly held off a battalion of Taliban by taking out the two lead vehicles of the column with a Barrett .50 caliber and then picking off the leaders one by one, sending the other troops scurrying for cover. Jared had held them off long enough for Brad and Ving to lead a gaggle of villagers and two wounded Marines to the safety of a convoy headed for Camp Leatherneck. As soon as they had turned the villagers and Marines over to the convoy commander, Brad and Ving had raced back toward Musa Qala and Jared, praying they would be in time to save their comrade, but not really believing they would.

Fearing the worst, they had reached Jared long before they got back to Musa Qala. They found him sitting cross-legged in a wadi surrounded by members of a patrol from the Army's 508th Parachute Infantry Regiment, giving an eloquent lecture on the art of making "cocoa-moco", his personal recipe for hot chocolate. The patrol leader had been in absolute awe of the rangy Marine sniper.

Brad was too busy focusing on the damned helicopter to tell Jess the story.

* * *

Leroy Harmon Jennings was a helluva chopper jockey. He had flown search and rescue and medevac missions for the Army in both Iraq and Afghanistan, over six hundred missions before he decided his luck was about to run out and retired. He had taken this job with the C.I.A. because it paid fantastic money and let him fly an assortment of

Company pukes around in relatively peaceful circumstances.

Whoever the hell people this asshat Waldingham was making him chase all around South Kalimantan were they were anything but peaceful. When he'd spotted them openly racing down the road to Sebamban, Waldingham had almost started frothing at the mouth, urging Jennings to get closer so the gunner could get a better shot at them. Jennings wasn't particularly fond of the asshat to begin with, but when he began ranting at the Company gunner to waste the people in the Mrazors, he really started to hate the puke. Hell, Jennings could clearly see that two of the passengers were women, and that really pissed him off. The people were shooting back, and Jennings couldn't find it in himself to fault them for that … but they were too good.

He had jerked the Huey up and away in a maneuver that nearly caused the asshat to fall to the deck of the chopper. That had made the asshat so angry that he had threatened to shoot Jennings, forgetting for the moment that Jennings was the only thing between him and a fiery death at the moment. Choppers don't fly themselves. Jennings had ignored the asshat after briefly considering shooting the bastard with the .45 he carried on his hip. He settled for keeping the chopper darting around like a ping-pong ball while asshat contacted the JI leader on his sat phone.

He shuddered as two more well-placed rounds penetrated the aluminum deck of the cargo compartment behind him. He rose another two hundred feet over the raucous objections of the asshat. Six more rounds struck the Huey, one shattering the left side of his Plexiglas windscreen. *Fuck asshat...* It was time to look for another job. He twisted the throttle and adjusted the pitch of the rotors, headed for the refueling area. If asshat didn't like it, he could get out and walk.

* * *

Where the hell did they come from? Jared wondered as he sighted down the bull barrel of his rifle. The scope was supposedly bore sighted, but he had not been able to check it. He estimated the distance to the two O.D. green vehicles roaring down the road towards him at about three hundred meters, and iron sights were good enough at that range. There had been no vehicles of this type at Camp Bashir, of that he was absolutely certain.

There was no way he could have known that Bintang Fadlhan had ordered a company of experienced Jemaah Islamiyah fighters into South Kalimantan as part of his secret, traitorous, and potentially hugely profitable conspiracy with Lawrence P. Waldingham III to take the Duckworth ransom money for themselves. Double crossing JI was an enormously risky proposition, but a hundred million dollars was worth the risk… The company had been spread out over several locations, including one that included a huge rubberized aviation fuel bladder for refueling the helicopter.

The lead vehicle looked for all the world like an old M-151 Army jeep, which it was. The trail vehicle was undoubtedly an old deuce and a half, which had been painted a dull yellow and put to use in a civilian logging operation before being commandeered by Jemaah Islamiyah.

Jared aimed at the windshield in front of the jeep driver, inhaled, then let half the breath back out, and then squeezed the trigger. A hole appeared in the windscreen in front of the driver's face and the vehicle swerved wildly before careening sideways and turning over on its side, wheels spinning. The driver of the deuce and a half locked up his brakes, but Jared had already sighted in on his windshield and fired once more.

The troops in the back of the truck were battle hardened, and it showed in the way they bailed out of the trucks and spread to both sides of the road. Jared unhurriedly picked out the ones who seemed to be leaders and began picking them off one at a time, slowing the orderly advance but not stopping it. These guys were not raw recruits.

* * *

Brad took a brief moment to look over his captive, who was now awake and glaring at him fiercely, hate plainly visible in his dark eyes. Checking the man's hands and feet to ensure that the bootlaces were still holding, Brad considered his next move. Where had the chopper gone? Satisfied that Hamdani wasn't going anywhere, he edged out to the side of the road and took in the results of Jared's handiwork.

The troops from the vehicles were spread out online still more than two hundred fifty meters away, firing their weapons steadily even though there was no way they could see what they were shooting at. They were executing a textbook suppression of fire maneuver. Brad's decision came swift and sure, from somewhere deep inside him. The chopper wasn't coming back. It was time to go.

He caught Ving's eye and gave him the signal to move out. Ving signaled to Pete and then gave out with a low whistle after Jared's latest shot. Jared glanced back, saw Ving's signal to move out, squeezed off one more round and then scurried back to the Mrazor on his belly.

"Through the forest until we get around the next bend," Brad said into the sat phone quietly. "Go slow, don't rev up the engines. With a little luck, it will take them a while to realize we're gone."

Ving, staring across the road at Brad, nodded his understanding and disconnected. "You heard?" he asked Jessica. She nodded and cranked the turbo diesel then eased her way through the forest about twenty meters into the wood line until she was sure she was past the next bend in the road. She stopped at the edge of the road until Ving's Mrazor appeared on the opposite side then eased out onto the unpaved surface and drove away as quietly as possible. Ving was right behind her.

Half a mile down the road, Brad signaled a halt and slid a hand across his throat. Jessica and Ving shut the engines off, and all of them strained to listen for the sound of engines. All they could hear was the sound of rifles being fired in a steady fashion off in the distance behind them.

"Let's get the hell outta Dodge," Brad said. The Mrazors' all-terrain tires threw rooster tails of mud up into the air as they sped away down the rough road, wide open.

* * *

They crossed two crude trestle bridges as they climbed toward the main mountain pass, and the terrible road was getting worse. It was obvious that the logging companies had stopped using the road some time before and had started taking their logs out by taking the southward route, avoiding both the difficult mountain pass and local police. The pain was fighting to escape its mental compartment, and Brad was flagging fast. He was finally beginning to feel that they had gotten clear of danger when they came to a washed out bridge.

The remains of the bridge lay in the water and appeared to have been there for several years. The water was shallow, and someone had clearly spread gravel across the bottom, preferring to ford rather than rebuild the bridge. If he had not been hurting so badly, he would never have made his next mistake. Clasping one hand over his aching side, he pumped his good arm in the signal to move out at speed.

They were all reaching the limit of their reserves, exhausted and ready to get the hell off of Borneo and back to Texas. Brad wasn't the only one whose focus was diminishing. They hit the water, throttles wide open and wheels sending great gouts of water into the air.

The leader of the ambush was unprepared for the remarkable speed of the Mrazors, and both vehicles were almost all the way across the stream before he initiated the ambush. His troops were concealed on both sides of the road, and because they were experienced veterans, they held their fire until the leader gave the signal. As a consequence, the Mrazor Jessica was driving slid up onto the roadway before its front wheels caught in a deep rut and it slewed violently to one side of the road and flipped over onto its side. Ving, taken by surprise, felt a bullet tug at the fabric of his shirt just before the front of his Mrazor clipped Jessica's and skidded to a stop.

Jared was the first one to react. Grabbing Duckworth by the collar of his shirt and charging through a hail of bullets, he took cover behind an enormous log that had fallen off a log truck at some time in the distant past.

The ambush party was having trouble executing their plan because the two Mrazors had passed through the kill zone and they did not wish to shoot their own people. They were now on the wrong side of their ambush, their detailed plan shot to hell. If not for their confusion, Team Dallas would have been annihilated.

The pain was blinding, and Brad was stunned, thrown from the front seat of the Mrazor. Jessica managed to release the buckle of her seat belt and crawl out the side, sobbing and calling for Charlie as she tried to get to Brad. Charlie appeared beside her and helped her to drag Brad further into the surrounding forest, the sound of sporadic gunfire filling their ears. Vicky had tried to get Hamdani's seat belt unfastened but gave it up as the ambushers began to get their shit together and their volume of fire picked up.

* * *

They had all miraculously managed to scuttle behind the massive Shorea log, and Brad and a terrified Duckworth were propped up with their backs against the soil that had drifted up against the log over the years it had lain in place.

"How many?" Brad grunted.

Jessica was tending to the two men, the other team members were scattered around the log, using its bulk to protect them from hostile fire. They were conserving ammo, careful not to fire unless they had a clear target. Even so, they were running out of ammo fast.

"I don't know, Brad, not as many as the last time I think," Jessica answered apprehensively. She had checked Duckworth, who had a through and through wound in his right thigh. It was still bleeding but slowly, the wound half cauterized by the passage of the high velocity .223 round. Brad's wound worried her. He had lost a tremendous amount of blood and he looked shocky. Worse yet, she had absolutely nothing to treat him with. Even the canteens holding their drinking water were in the cargo area on the overturned Mrazor.

"Go." Brad waved her hands away from him. "We need all the shooters we can get." Despite the obvious seriousness of his wound and Jessica's protests, he struggled to a kneeling position. "Where's my rifle?"

"Jesus, Brad, it's not like I had time to hunt down your rifle when we wrecked. You're in no condition to fight anyway, you don't look good."

He gave her an exhausted smile.

"If we don't come up with some kind of miracle, it's not going to make any difference, Jess." He drew the .45 from its holster and poked his head and arm around the thick end of the log. His vision was a little blurry, but he rested his arm against the butt end of the log and waited until he found a target. Aiming center mass, he squeezed off a round and the big pistol bucked in his hand. The target dropped like a sack of potatoes.

Jessica knew her cousin was a stubborn cuss and that, no matter what she said, he would keep fighting. She reached down and picked up her M-16, ejecting the magazine and checking to see how many rounds she had left. Not many. She gazed longingly at the overturned Mrazor, only twenty feet away, where the canvas pouch containing the spare magazines hung from the roll cage. She wondered briefly if she was fast enough to reach the damned thing before somebody plugged her. A fusillade of bullets from the other side of the road forced her to duck behind the log.

* * *

Ving lay prone, making sure he had a clear target and taking careful aim before squeezing off each round. He had checked his magazine already, there were a dozen rounds left besides the one spare thirty-round mag in his pocket. He patted the pocket to reassure himself, but inwardly he wondered if he would ever see Jordan and Nathaniel again. He was extremely grateful to Willona for sending them on that fishing trip to Grapevine Lake. It was beginning to look as if there might never be another.

* * *

Jared and Pete lay side by side in a natural depression off to the right side of the fallen log, firing methodically at the ambushers as soon as one gave them a clear target, which was not as often as they'd have liked. The hostiles were pretty savvy, not at all like the recruits they had encountered at Camp Bashir.

"I kinda wish we'd set that kid free before we left," Pete said soberly, taking careful aim and then taking his finger off the trigger as his target ducked down behind a log of his own.

"Not to worry," Jared grunted as he dropped another hostile. "I loosened his bonds before we left. He'll work his way out of them before long. I just hope he doesn't get caught by those cadre members. I've heard horror stories…"

Pete thought about the kid for a second, and then his mind returned to the situation at hand.

"I've got two fully charged mags left, how are yours holding out?"

Jared didn't have to look; he always knew how much ammo he was carrying, an occupational necessity for a dedicated sniper.

"Sixty rounds, plus what I have in this mag."

"How many of them are there?"

"I make it about sixteen left … not as many as we held off back near the O.R.P."

"You mean *you* held off," Pete said pointedly.

Jared ignored the comment. He simply waited for another head to pop up; just like an old-fashioned turkey shoot back in Texas—and that gave him an idea.

NINETEEN

No one had to tell Brad the team was running low on ammunition, and he knew that every member was fully aware that there would be no cavalry rushing in to rescue them... They were not only all alone in a foreign country, they would be considered mercenaries by the government if they were caught. Nobody really wanted them here except Duckworth, and, at the moment, he was as powerless as they were.

He knew he didn't need to call attention to their ammunition shortage, they were all experienced enough to know what a hell of a fix they were in. Fire discipline was good, and everyone seemed to be picking their shots. Fighting back the pain, he struggled to come up with a solution to the problem, but the only thing he could come up with was checking to see how many of the seven-round .45 magazines they were carrying. It wasn't much, but it was all he had ... and they would soon be down to the .45s.

* * *

Jared carefully considered his options, and the only idea he could come up with was one he had heard from his grandfather when he was just a kid back in Abilene. His grandpa had been telling a tale around a campfire, Jared couldn't remember the occasion. The talk around the fire had turned to tales of the Old West, and Grandpa had regaled them with a story about his own grandfather, who had fought the Comanche way back in the day.

The way Grandpa told it, his grandfather, Hezekiah Smoot, had found himself alone in the desert of West Texas after getting separated from his cavalry troop during a sandstorm. Hezekiah hadn't been in the Army, he had been a contract scout for the cavalry, and he had been the possessor of a unique rifle invented by a Mr. Christopher Spencer. The rifle, a magazine-fed, lever-action rifle was chambered for the .56-56 Spencer rimfire cartridge. The tubular magazine carried seven rounds that could be fired as fast as the hammer could be manually cocked.

Hezekiah had walked into an arroyo hunting something to eat, toting that rifle and carrying a handful of spare cartridges in his pocket. He had not noticed the Comanche on the lip of the arroyo until he had stumbled right into their midst. He had raced for cover, hiding from the pissed off warriors as best he could. They had the advantage of numbers over him, but Hezekiah was armed with something the Comanche had never seen and wouldn't be able to understand if they had. He was also blessed with an overabundance of audacity. The long and the short of the story was that Hezekiah had crept from boulder to boulder, from draw to ridge, picking off the warriors by firing his rifle when they fired their stolen cavalry carbines at whatever distraction he came up with. One shot, one kill ... a family tradition.

Jared knew he had no other options available. Brad, the only other team member who could match him, could barely move. Ving, as stealthy a man as one of those Comanche that Grandpa had told him about, was just too damned big to conceal his bulk in broad daylight. Pete was a good man with a gun, and no slouch as a recon man, was a pilot by trade for God's sake. He couldn't match Jared or Ving in fieldcraft. Good as they were, he wouldn't even consider Jessica or Vicky. He was willing to admit that he was being chauvinistic, but he wasn't about to stay behind a damned log while a girl went out to do a job he was most qualified for and most experienced at. No, this job was for him and him alone.

"Pete!"

"Yeah?"

"Would you slip over behind that log and divvy up the ammo? Make sure everybody has the same number of rounds?"

"What the hell? What are you up to, Jared?"

"Just trust me, Pete, and don't give me any shit."

He didn't like it one little bit, but Pete was a team player and Jared had proved himself trustworthy more times than Pete could count. He would do as Jared asked, but he wasn't happy about it. He turned his back on Jared and began the slow, laborious crawl over to the others. He never saw Jared slither out of the depression and begin to make his way to the far right side of the line of hostiles without disturbing so much as a blade of grass.

* * *

The hostiles had apparently figured out that Team Dallas was shooting anyone who exposed any part of their body because the shooting had nearly stopped, a circumstance Jared thought of as a Mexican standoff. The heat was almost unbearable, the sun beating down on all of them unmercifully. Sweat poured off Jared in rivers, but he ignored it. The rainforest was unnaturally silent, the animals and most of the insects scared away by the gunshots and the smell of cordite. Occasionally a branch would fall or a cone would fall with a sound that seemed as loud as a hand grenade exploding. It had been a long time since Jared had attempted an infiltration in broad daylight.

He measured his progress toward the last position he had spotted one of the shooters in mere centimeters, the ultimate sniper challenge. Midmorning came and still the hostiles had taken no action, which Jared found odd, but he kept moving anyway. The tree trunk where he had last seen the shooter was only twenty feet away.

*   *   *

The leader of the ambush team, Fauzi Atmadja, was a very junior *Sersan* (sergeant) in Jemaah Islamiyah. *Tuan* Fadlhan had promoted him personally, and his new subordinates had assumed (quite rightly) that he had been promoted more because he was a distant relation of the *Tuan* than because it was merited. The promotion had its perks, but it had its drawbacks as well. *Tuan* Fadlhan was well known for his vicious temper and his cruelty. He was also very powerful within the organization, and his transgressions were most often overlooked by his superiors for that reason.

Fadlhan's evil reputation was the primary reason for the stalemate. The rest of the reason was Atmadja's inexperience. He had been ecstatic when he had seen the Americans approaching the river, but he had been surprised by the speed of the weird looking vehicles they were using. He was no stranger to ATVs, but he had never seen any like these. He had been caught by surprise by the lightning speed at the ford, and the ATVs had managed to get all the way across the river before he could collect his wits and initiate the ambush.

As a result, the Americans had gotten behind his troops, leaving their backs to the river. The Amis were far too clever too. They had limited their fire to direct responses, costing Atmadja seven of the nineteen fighters he had brought with him.

Atmadja had finally ordered a halt to the shooting, unwilling to proceed until he could figure out a way to get at the Amis and kill them. He dared not fail on his first mission, *Tuan* would have him skinned alive in front of the company if he failed this simple mission. Atmadja was rethinking his commitment to Jemaah Islamiyah instead of putting his mind to the solution of the problem ... and his fighters were beginning to lose their enthusiasm. They'd already lost what little respect they'd had for him.

* * *

"What's taking him so long?" Jessica whispered.

"He's going to take out the shooters one at a time," Brad whispered back. It was an educated guess; he knew Jared better than anyone, except perhaps Ving, and he knew how the man thought. "We've got to stay alert. If I understand this correctly, he's going to send us a signal of some kind when he makes his move, and we're going to have to create a diversion for him, a good one."

"Yeah," Ving whispered. "I just hope he starts soon." He mopped the sweat off his forehead with the back of his hand. "Whatever he does, I guarantee all hell is gonna break loose when he does it."

* * *

The last shooter was lying face down, his head resting on his hands, his M-16 on the ground beside him. Jared had circled around behind him, checking the area around the guy for the next shooter in the line. This one had made two mistakes. He had failed to maintain visual contact with the next shooter in line, and he had allowed himself to drowse instead of staying alert in the heat. It was the last mistake he would ever make.

Jared coiled himself like a rattlesnake, every muscle in his body tense and ready to explode. Then he noiselessly launched himself through the short distance between them, combat knife in hand. He covered the shooter's mouth with one hand and plunged the knife between the third and fourth ribs on the left side of his spine, piercing the heart from behind. The shooter died without ever knowing he was being attacked.

Jared rolled the man over, avoiding looking at the wide-open eyes as he checked the man's body for magazines. Nothing. Patient and thorough, Jared lifted a canvas sack from the ground beside the M-16 and found a half dozen fully charged magazines. The fortunate discovery called for a re-evaluation of his plan, but there wasn't much time. There was no telling when the leader of the shooters might suddenly get his shit together and check his men. Jared took the man's black cotton shirt and carefully packed it around the magazines so that they wouldn't rattle against each other, and then he slung the nearly new looking M-16 over the dead man's chest and closed his eyes so that he appeared to be sleeping. Then he silently slunk back into the forest, this time *behind* the line of shooters.

* * *

"This is getting old, Brad. I still think I should go around the other side of the line and start takin' 'em out the way Jared plans to. Hell, we don't even know he ain't already been caught."

The words had barely left Pete's mouth when the little red light on Brad's sat phone began to blink and the silence of the rainforest was shattered by the sound of an M-16 on full automatic. All of them peered over the log and saw the shooters frantically clawing their way around the cover they had been hiding behind and looking for the source of the gunfire. Several of them never made it.

"Go!" Brad bellowed as he staggered to his feet and began to move towards the shooters, his .45 in his hand.

The team sprinted past the Mrazors, firing what was left of their M-16 rounds, and closed with the remnants of the ambush team, .45s blazing. It was over in seconds, and Jared joined them before the echoes from the gunfire died out in the forest.

Brad's muscles had stiffened up over the long period of inactivity and it was all over before he managed to limp painfully over to his team. Vicky took one look at him and raced back to the overturned Mrazor to get his canteen.

"Duckworth?" Brad asked thickly. Pete and Jessica sprinted back to the log they had used for cover to retrieve the oilman, and Brad watched Pete stop and kneel down beside Hamdani, who was still strapped into the back seat of the overturned Mrazor.

"Damn," Vicky exclaimed. "I didn't even check on that bastard."

"Doesn't look like he's moved since we turned it over," Brad croaked, taking a sip from the canteen Vicky had handed him. He fought the urge to drink deeply, certain that gorging himself with water would make him puke. He was feeling decidedly unwell.

Pete stood up and shook his head.

"Dead," he remarked unnecessarily. Hamdani's body was riddled with bullets, making all of them wonder why none of them had been hit.

"Leave him strapped in," Brad rasped. He had an idea of a way to use the corpse to their advantage, no matter how obscene it might be.

"Duckworth's a little shocky, but he's going to be okay," Jessica announced, standing up from behind the log and flashing them a thumbs up sign. Pete stepped around behind the log and a moment later the two came out with Duckworth supported between them.

"Somebody shot me," Duckworth muttered. His features changed as his overloaded mind shifted gears. "I don't mean to sound ungrateful, but do you suppose I could get some water to drink?" He watched Jessica as she let go of him and ran over to the Mrazor to retrieve her own canteen. "I feel a little dizzy," he said, a blank look on his face.

"Okay, he's more than a little shocky," Jessica muttered, once more taking the man's hand and guiding him toward Ving's Mrazor.

"Let's get that thing rolled over and see if we can get it started," Brad said. "We need to get the hell outta here."

*   *   *

Righting the overturned Mrazor turned out to be easier said than done. They were all weakened and exhausted, none of them had slept in forty-eight hours, and none of them had eaten anything other than a couple of energy bars in the same time period. Several minutes of straining and lifting failed to get the damned thing back on its wheels. Even the massive muscles of Ving and Pete didn't help.

"Why don't we just use the winch?" Vicky asked. Even the handcuffed Duckworth was stunned.

"Dammit girl!" Ving grumbled. He turned to Brad. "Why didn't we think of that?"

Ving started his Mrazor easily, but when he tried to back away from Brad's Mrazor, they found that the winch was wedged between the rear deck support and the left rear wheel.

"Shit!"

"It ain't nothin' to cuss about, Ving," Pete said, rummaging around beneath the seat for a lug wrench or a tire tool. He grinned and drew out a metal bar. "I got this!"

While Pete struggled to separate the two vehicles, Vicky worked at the handcuffs on Duckworth's wrists.

"Almost there," she said, her tongue poking out between her teeth as she concentrated. "Your wrists are rubbed raw. You must have made a terrific effort to get out of these things."

"Where is my driver?" Duckworth muttered. He looked around him uncomprehendingly. "Who are you people?"

There was the sound of the inner mechanism of the cuffs clicking and one side of the cuffs popped open.

"There," Vicky said with a wry smile. She turned to Jessica. "He's really out of it. Normally you treat for shock by keeping the victim warm and elevating their feet, but what do you do for them when it's already hot as hell?"

"Just keep giving him water, Vicky, that's all I can figure."

There was a muted clang from the Mrazors and the winch sprang free of the overturned Mrazor.

"Done!" Pete tossed the bar back onto the floorboard and waved for Ving to back away from the overturned Mrazor. He reeled out enough of the cable so that he could attach the hook on the end to the lifting eye at the base of the center support of the roll cage.

"Wind it up, Ving!"

Ving flicked the toggle on the control box on the console to "low" and the winch began to take up cable. The powerful winch made short work of the task, and in seconds the Mrazor was teetering on two wheels. The vehicle slammed down onto all four wheels and bounced twice.

"Saddle up!" Brad barked, his voice a little steadier than it had been earlier. In a matter of seconds, Team Dallas, an injured Duckworth, and a dead terrorist were racing back down the road for Sebamban. Vicky was trying to give Duckworth water from Jessica's canteen, and Pete had transferred to the lead Mrazor to even out the loads.

* * *

The heat, the food deprivation, the lack of sleep, and, most of all, the pain and blood loss had depleted Brad's reserves drastically, but this was not the first time he had been in a bad way. He had long before learned that the human body was capable of surviving far more abuse than people could comprehend. True toughness came from within, from the mind, from the sheer will to survive. At that moment, however, survival was not enough. His team, the people he cared about most in the world, depended on his ability to be a functional member of the team. It would take the combined skills and abilities of the team to get past the final obstacles to the successful completion of their mission.

He forced his mind to ignore the pain, pushing it back into its mental compartment. The jouncing of the Mrazor was making him nauseous, but he swallowed that back, fighting for control of his stomach. It was a battle he won but just barely. He struggled to raise his canteen to his lips and managed to take another tiny sip. He knew that hydration was critical at this point, both for the loss of water through perspiration and breathing and for the blood loss. He finally managed to get his body under some semblance of control as he practiced the deep breathing technique he had used earlier.

The helicopter had left them in the rainforest, but he still didn't know why. It was possible that the chopper had taken a hit that made it necessary to cease flight operations or possibly one of the occupants had taken a serious hit and required immediate medical attention, he just didn't know. What he did know was that the C.I.A. wasn't done with Team Dallas yet. Whatever that asshole Waldingham was up to, there was no way he was going to just give up. The question in Brad's mind was whether he had something Waldingham wanted badly enough to trade for their freedom.

* * *

They were making for the coast, staying on the main road to Sebamban and pushing the Mrazors to their limit over the treacherous, rutted road. The time for subtlety and stealth was behind them. Throwing all caution to the wind, they were relying on speed and surprise to get them to the coast.

Bracing himself against the seat in front of him, Brad managed to extract his secure satellite phone from the cargo pocket on his right thigh. It was hard to get his eyes to focus well enough to see the numbers on the phone clearly.

"Give me that, Brad." Jared reached for the phone and glanced at his friend and leader. "Herb?" he asked. Brad nodded. Inwardly he was praying that Pete's buddy's brother had not already departed for Jakarta and left them in the lurch. Jared checked the "Contacts" section and selected the speed dial number for the pilot of the PBM-5.

* * *

When Herb had left Team Dallas on the beach near Sebamban, he had flown at wave top level so that he didn't show up on radar anywhere near where he had dropped the team off. After the short flight, he had landed his seaplane in the Siring Park Sea, off Taman Siring Laut, 50-odd miles north-northeast of their initial LZ. Brad Jacobs had paid him to wait seventy-two hours, and Herb had no intention of leaving without the man.

When the call came, it was hard to hear… Jacobs sounded funny, but perhaps that was because Herb was running from the hammock he had set up on the beach toward Louise. Like the good, old pilot that he was, Herb did not rush his preflight inspection. He could do Team Dallas no good if he dumped Louise in the drink on his way to pick them up or when he was completing the extraction. Thirty minutes later, he was screaming just above the whitecaps, pushing Louise to her absolute limit.

* * *

"You don't look so good, brother," Ving said. They had reached the extraction point without further incident, but the team was scouring the tree line for any sign of pursuers. Despite their exultation at the prospect of their imminent extraction, they were all on edge.

When they had first arrived on the beach, Brad had directed them to the relative concealment of the row of hardwood trees just inside the row of palms that lined the beach. When they had finished scouting the area, they returned to the Mrazor where Brad sat staring out over the blue waves of the Java Sea and Jessica sat tending to Duckworth, who was showing definite signs of improvement.

With some difficulty, Brad managed to turn in his seat and look at the still body of Hamdani, whom he still couldn't put a name to. He knew the man was important, and probably a leader, but he had no idea whether the dead man was important enough to be of any benefit to the team. He said so aloud, mostly to himself, but his half-mumbled utterance spurred Pete to action.

The big man lumbered over to where Hamdani's body sat, grotesquely upright, in the rearmost seat of Ving's Mrazor. He unfastened the seat belt holding the corpse up and then eased it out onto the sand, where he began a thorough search of its clothing as the others watched him.

"Glad he did that instead of me," Ving remarked with a wry smile.

"I should have thought of it sooner…"

"You've had enough on your mind, Brad," Vicky retorted. She was worried about him. She was a remarkable woman, and she had a high tolerance for her own pain. She was finding it difficult, however, dealing with the pain of someone she cared deeply about. Falling in love with Brad Jacobs had altered her professional demeanor in ways she had never anticipated, and she wasn't certain how to deal with these new feelings.

A cry of surprise came from Pete after he rolled Hamdani's corpse over and located a small leather case in the rear pocket of the body's trousers.

"What did you find?" Charlie asked anxiously, walking hesitantly toward Pete.

"Looks like one of them diplomatic carnets," Pete muttered as he opened it and took out a plasticized identity card. He stared at it in puzzlement. "Says here his name is Ahmad Hamdani."

"Jesus, let me see that," Charlie exclaimed, hurrying over to stand beside Pete. He compared the face on the card with the face of the corpse. "I can't be sure, guys, I can't remember his face, but the name is familiar enough. If this is really him, the guy is responsible for blowing up shit all over the freakin' world, going back to the failed World Trade Center bombing in the early '90s. Christ, he's wanted by virtually every law enforcement agency in the damned world."

Brad was skeptical, but he felt a glimmer of hope anyway.

"You think?" he asked rhetorically. Then his face dropped. "Why would a wanted man carry a real identity card around with him?"

Jared shrugged.

"Ego maybe? Who knows?

"It doesn't matter!" Charlie said excitedly. "We have a dead body, we have what looks like a legitimate Indonesian I.D. card bearing the face of a wanted terrorist ... and we can use that as a bargaining chip!"

"I'm not sure I follow you," Brad remarked. His mind was getting fuzzy again.

"Daniel! I can call Daniel!" Charlie wanted to say more, but he stopped when he saw Brad's head loll to one side as he passed out.

"We need to get him to a hospital ASAP," Vicky said worriedly, holding two fingers against Brad's jugular vein. "He's lost too much blood." She checked the nylon strap keeping pressure on the wound, but there was nothing she could do to make it better.

* * *

"Man, I don't know, but it looks like it's your only shot," Daniel Novianti said into the other end of the connection. "I just don't think it's gonna slow Waldingham at all, if he gets there before you guys can get on that airplane he's going to come in shooting. I don't know exactly what happened, but he's mad as hell and out for blood. My boss is *still* giving me shit."

"How far out is he?"

"I'm guessing about an hour, according to what my boss just said."

"That will have to be enough, Daniel." Charlie disconnected the call. Louise had splashed down and was idling towards the beach. "We may have to leave the Mrazors here on the beach," he called out. "We have less than an hour before Waldingham gets here."

"Oh *HELL* no," Ving retorted, cranking up his Mrazor and driving it out onto the open sound. "No way in hell I'm gonna take my black ass back to Dallas and tell Ms. Willona I left these two-thirty-thousand-dollar toys on some godforsaken beach in Borneo…"

"You heard the man," Jared said with a grin. "I don't relish the idea of a Willona Ving ass-chewin' either. That is the sweetest woman in the world, but I'd rather low-crawl nekkid across twenty acres of broke glass than have to face that woman when she's pissed."

Pete chuckled, climbing into the driver's seat of the other Mrazor and cranking it up.

"That boy does have a colorful way of talkin', but I get his drift. I'll take my chances of Waldingham showing up. I can shoot back at him."

They left Hamdani's body on the beach.

* * *

With considerable difficulty, they managed to load Brad's unconscious form aboard Louise and Vicky set about making him as comfortable as possible on the deck right behind the cockpit. The rest of the team, under the watchful eyes of Herb himself, managed to load the Mrazors back aboard the plane and secure them to the cargo floor in record time. They kicked the ramps off the doorframe and let them fall to the sand rather than waste time securing them to the cargo deck.

"Secure those to the deck and make damned sure they're tight!" yelled Herb over the roar of the engines. "The last thing I need is one of them coming loose during takeoff!"

Within half an hour of the end of Charlie's conversation with Daniel Novianti, there was nothing left on the beach besides the tracks left by

Louise's wheels and hungry raptors eyeing the corpse of Ahmad Hamdani.

* * *

A thoroughly disgusted Lawrence P. Waldingham III stood beneath the blazing sun staring down at Ahmad Hamdani, wondering if he would end up in the same condition sometime in the near future. Waldingham kicked the body viciously, furious.

"All you had to do was hold on to Duckworth for *one more fucking day!*" He had put his future with the C.I.A. in jeopardy by accepting Fadlhan's offer, bribe really, of a substantial chunk of the Duckworth ransom money for keeping anyone from repatriating the oil magnate. He had no idea why his bosses at the C.I.A. had wanted to keep Brad Jacobs and his team from getting to the Texan, but he had failed them too. The last thought he had before the bullet entered the back of his head was that he might have an outside chance of getting the Company to transfer him out of theater if he could figure out a way to take credit for the death of Hamdani, who was high on the World's Most Wanted List. He was dead wrong.

The copilot of the black Huey holstered his Beretta 92F and climbed back into the cockpit and gave the signal for takeoff to the new guy who had replaced Leroy Jennings. He was going to miss Jennings. The guy had been a hell of a chopper jockey and a real nice guy.

TWENTY

Despite the need to get the team out of Indonesia altogether, Vicky had convinced Herb that Brad would never survive the flight back to Jakarta without medical treatment. Herb had pushed Louise to her limits getting across the Makassar Strait to West Sulawesi, where he had a cousin working in a village clinic for Doctors Without Borders.

The doctor had been nervous, concerned about Herb's insistence on not notifying the authorities, but Herb was blood kin. This relationship and Brad's condition had finally decided the issue. Ving had informed the doctor that he and Brad shared the same blood type, but the doctor had typed them both anyway. When he got the results, he ordered Ving up on a gurney and an orderly moved it beside the bed where Brad lay unconscious.

As the orderly wiped Ving's arm down with an alcohol pad, Ving rolled his head to one side and stared at his friend.

"You don't know it yet, brother, but when this is over, you gonna owe me the biggest bacon sammich East Texas has ever seen."

Vicky didn't know whether to laugh or cry.

* * *

Bill Duckworth, fresh from a tepid shower and dressed in nondescript khaki clothing, rested in a wheelchair and stared with undisguised respect at the gorgeous redhead who just explained to him what had happened since he'd been taken in Brunei.

"And it was just the seven of you against all the terrorists?" he asked again in disbelief.

"It wasn't as bad as it sounded," Vicky said modestly.

Duckworth glanced over at Brad, still lying on the primitive hospital bed.

"I think he might tend to disagree with you, young lady," he said weakly. Duckworth had regained most of his mental clarity, but the doctor had told them the man wasn't up to an extended flight.

"You just wait until he wakes up, Mr. Duckworth; he'll be the first to tell you this was just business as usual."

Duckworth was bone-tired, weary, and weak. His thigh throbbed painfully where the bullet had torn through his leg. The ravishing auburn-haired beauty who had greeted him sweetly when he had come to had raised his spirits considerably, but he was not some yokel off the streets of Midland, Texas. He knew very well the power and reach of Jemaah Islamiyah, and he knew that in some quarters within the government of the Sultanate of Brunei, as well as in Washington, D.C., the multi-billion dollar private deal he had been about to sign with the deputy minister for energy and industry would have met with violent opposition. In retrospect, he realized that the opposition was more violent than he'd anticipated. He'd expected anger and political ranting. He'd not expected to be kidnapped and probably even murdered. He hung his head for a moment, gathering his strength.

"You cannot even imagine how grateful I am, young lady. I just don't ... have the words."

"You don't have to say anything at all, Mr. Duckworth. This is what we do," Vicky said simply.

* * *

Pete's satellite phone had the most battery power left, so Bill Duckworth borrowed it and found a quiet place to make a call, a call that lasted until the lithium battery pack was almost exhausted. When he was finished, he gave it back to Pete gratefully. Then he had Vicky summon Herb.

"My associate, Howard Grainger, tells me that our corporate jet is undergoing minor repairs half a world away and it will be a couple of days before it can get here. What I need to know, sir, is how long it will take you to get us to Jakarta?"

"From here?" Herb asked. He scratched his chin and thought for a moment. "Somewhere between four and five hours, depending on whether we catch a headwind."

"I have an office in Jakarta, Mr. Wilcox. When we land there, we will be met by an officer of Duckworth International Petroleum bearing a check in the amount of twenty-five thousand dollars."

Herb was a businessman but not a greedy one.

"Mr. Duckworth, Brad already paid me for this gig—"

"Nevertheless, I am grateful for what you have already done, and I am afraid I do not trust any of the other operators in this part of the world to transport us at the moment. You realize, of course, that there are governments involved in this fiasco, do you not?"

"I do."

"Then you know that the danger your friends have faced is not over yet. With that in mind, are you still willing to fly us to Jakarta?"

"Of course I am," Herb said indignantly. "A contract is a contract. Besides, Pete and my brother are tight, and any man my brother will vouch for is a friend of mine."

"Then an additional fee is justified, Mr. Wilcox."

* * *

The doctor had not been happy about letting Brad fly to Jakarta in his condition, but he had been concerned about problems with Sulawesian authorities so he had acceded to Ving's demands for release ... that and he did not wish to disturb the bald, muscular black man who carried a rather wicked looking pistol on his hip and constantly and loudly complained about the dearth of bacon in Sulawesi.

Duckworth eased the doctor's anxieties considerably when he advised that a generous donation from Duckworth International Petroleum would be immediately forthcoming.

The flight to Jakarta was smooth as silk, though it took longer because Herb skirted a patch of bad weather to avoid possible turbulence. He used the extra time to patch his radio through to a landline and arrange for his wife to have an ambulance and a doctor meet Louise and transport Brad and Duckworth to a private hospital. Howard Grainger had made arrangements for a security detail from Duckworth International Petroleum's Jakarta office to meet them and escort the team until they could be spirited out of Jakarta. He had also arranged for the private hospital to allow the security team to attend the two patients. Money had an amazing ability to ease restrictions imposed on people of lesser means.

* * *

Bill Duckworth insisted on being put in the same room with Brad, who had been fitted with a plasma I.V. in West Sulawesi after receiving whole blood from Ving. Brad's recovery had been swift and damned near miraculous.

The doctors had removed the stitches he'd received in West Sulawesi, abraded and cleaned the wound, treating it with the latest in antibiotics before stapling it back together. The pain was manageable, which was great because Brad refused anything stronger than the Tylenol 3, which was the least powerful pain reliever the doctors were willing to give him.

He had started feeling much better as soon as the anesthetic wore off, and he had been pleased that Duckworth was so grateful, but the man's gratitude quickly became cloying and embarrassing. Even Vicky's presence and the constant visits by Ving and the others didn't slow down the constant flow of praise and thanks.

Vicky took advantage of a brief respite when the security detail (minus one hard looking man who was obviously packing who remained in the room with Brad) went with the orderlies who wheeled Duckworth down to X-ray.

"Calm yourself, Brad, he's just really grateful. This whole ordeal has been like something out of an action movie for him. He's just overwhelmed," she whispered.

"He's driving me nuts," Brad whispered back.

"His company is paying you more than you made all last year," Vicky retorted, a little louder. Brad shut his mouth and a sheepish look crept across his face. Vicky tried to suppress a laugh but she couldn't. Then she hugged him so hard he flinched in pain ... but he didn't say anything. Vicky's hugs were not something he wanted to discourage.

* * *

Brad was worried. He needed to get himself out of the hospital and the team out of Indonesia. There had been no official fallout from the mission; he supposed he should be grateful to Duckworth International Petroleum's battery of international lawyers for that. He was certain that the longer the team stayed in-country the greater their chances of being interrogated and taken into custody would become.

* * *

Duckworth, grateful beyond words, had Grainger arrange to have the Mrazors air-freighted back to Dallas at his own expense. Then he invited the team to travel back home with him on his corporate jet. The jet was a gleaming new Gulfstream G650, and no expense had been spared on the custom interior. Lustrous leather seats that fully reclined, gleaming exotic wood furnishings and brass fittings were the order of the day.

An extremely attractive blonde flight attendant tried to serve them champagne, but when Ving politely declined, she offered to bring him a Lone Star beer, which he gladly accepted once she told him there was plenty of bacon aboard and she would be pleased to make him a "sammich". By the time the Gulfstream landed in Dallas, she would have a new definition for the word "plenty".

She had better luck with Jared, who she seemed to be very interested in and who was delighted to regale her with the proper way to concoct his "cocoa-moco".

Duckworth had bumped the attorneys to a commercial flight, allowing only his personal physician and a quartet of somber security men to make the return flight. Team Dallas was being given the royal treatment.

TWENTY-ONE

The Gulfstream landed at Dallas-Fort Worth International and taxied to the Duckworth International Petroleum's private hangar. The hangar was as impressive as the Gulfstream and just as lavishly appointed.

"I have never seen a damned mechanic that clean before," Ving remarked as an army of uniformed workmen descended on the shiny aircraft bearing a baffling array of tools, gadgets, and cleaning implements. They were surprisingly quiet as they worked, well organized, and extremely efficient.

"Oh Lord," Ving exclaimed. "We gotta get outta here before Willona sees these people workin'!" He turned and started walking toward the hangar office. A couple of the bodyguards had trundled Duckworth there in a wheelchair as soon as he had gotten off the jet. Duckworth's physician had attempted to insist that Brad be wheeled out, too, and there had even been a chair brought out for him by one of the workmen, but Brad had flatly rejected the idea.

"I don't need a wheelchair," he had stubbornly insisted. He had made it all the way to the bottom of the exit stairs before he stumbled and almost fell, causing him to stretch his wound and grimace in pain. Vicky instantly slipped herself beneath the arm on his good side, trying to make it appear as if Brad had done it out of familiar affection.

Jessica recognized what had happened, but she didn't say anything. She had thought she understood her cousin's pride better than anyone, but she felt a new admiration for the redhead's intuition and quick thinking. Jared, at the top of the steps, had noticed what happened as well, and he turned and went back inside the aircraft. Brad was still standing at the base of the stairs, pretending to watch the workmen, when he returned carrying a cane and a tube of something that looked like toothpaste. He thrust the cane at Brad.

"You should probably use this," he said, slipping the tube unobtrusively to Vicky with his free hand. "Don't want to get Duckworth in trouble with his insurance company, do we?"

"What the hell, Jared?" Brad seemed irate.

Jared inclined his head toward one of the uniformed workmen who was wearing a yellow hat instead of a white one like the rest of the crew.

"Dollar to a donut he's a union steward, buddy."

Reluctantly, Brad removed his arm from around Vicky's shoulder and took the proffered cane. He turned and made slow, painful progress toward the hangar office.

"Topical anesthetic," Jared whispered to Vicky, flicking his eyes down at the tube in her hand. "Doc said just rub it over the staples and keep an eye on the wound to make sure he doesn't pull them loose." Vicky gave him a small grateful smile and hurried after her man.

* * *

Bill Duckworth had a large, opulent office adjoining the hangar office that he obviously used when he didn't have time to go to his headquarters downtown between flights. There were doors leading to a bedroom and a bar on the side wall of the office. Duckworth had been rolled into the bar. The security man had rolled him up to a highly polished mahogany bar with a shiny brass footrail and then stepped behind the bar. He had taken a bottle of twenty-five-year-old Macallan Scotch from the mirrored shelf behind the bar and set it down beside a tray of squat tumblers.

"Get another bottle from under the bar, Jason," Duckworth had commanded. "Make sure there's enough for everyone."

Jason splashed about three fingers of the expensive single malt scotch into eight of the tumblers, and then Duckworth had indicated he should pour another one for himself.

Duckworth raised his tumbler solemnly.

"To Team Dallas!" He drained the tumbler in a single gulp and then watched as everyone took a sip.

"I've had a lot of time to think about this on our flight home," he said slowly. "There's no way I can ever thank you enough for what you've done for me…"

"Mr. Duckworth—" Brad started, but the older man raised a hand, palm outward to stop him.

"Never interrupt a man who's thanking you for being the best at what you do, son, it's unseemly. Now, as I was saying, there's no way I can ever thank you enough for what you did for me, so I had

Howard do a little checking for me, and I think I've come up with a little something concrete to better show my gratitude."

"Mr. Duckworth, we try to give our best on every mission we take on. Willona negotiated a pretty stiff fee for this mission, and while we appreciate your desire to be generous, we're perfectly happy with the agreed upon fee."

Duckworth gave him a stony stare.

"Do you have any idea how much Duckworth International Petroleum made last year, son?"

"No sir, I don't."

"Last year we *netted* a little over thirty billion dollars, and I personally took twenty percent off the top. Now, I don't usually pull dumbass stunts that put my life in danger, I have a very efficient security team that usually accompanies me wherever I go. This time I got too big for my britches, thought I could keep what I was doing a secret from everybody in the world by taking a commercial flight and not traveling with a bunch of guys packing guns who look like they could fight off a small army. I was wrong."

He held out his glass for more of the Macallan and Jason poured another three fingers for him. Duckworth tossed it back like it was water. He smacked his lips and set the tumbler down on the bar.

"As I was saying, I was wrong, and because I made a foolish mistake, you people had to wade into a special part of hell to bring my dumb ass home. The fee Mrs. Ving negotiated doesn't amount to even one percent of my monthly salary, and that didn't strike me as fair compensation for a job well done, especially a job that kept my ass alive." He thumped his fist on the arm of the wheelchair for emphasis.

He glanced over at a clock on the wall.

"I decided to do something about that to show my appreciation. Howard Grainger will be here in a minute to take you to Mrs. Ving, and I want you folks to go with him when she gets here. Consider it the final step in your rescue mission." He motioned for Jason to come around from the back of the bar.

"I thank you, folks, from the bottom of my heart, and I wish I could go with you, but I have to get back aboard the jet when the maintenance crew is finished with her. I've got to go straighten out the mess I've made of this deal, but this time Jason and his compatriots are going with me."

* * *

Team Dallas did not have to stand outside to wait for Grainger after all. He arrived moments after Duckworth took his leave, driving inside the hangar and up to the office door in a spanking new Ford Excursion painted a deep, shiny black.

Uniformed employees rushed to open the doors for them.

"Climb on in," Grainger said by way of greeting. "There wasn't time to even take the plastic covers off the seats." The big SUV had that unmistakable new car smell.

"Where are you takin' us?" Ving asked, eyeing the slick, well-dressed oil executive with suspicion.

"Why, I'm taking you to see your wife, Mr. Ving," Grainger said pleasantly. "Just sit back and enjoy the scenery. I apologize ahead of time for the length of the ride, but the helicopter wasn't available. Carson has it in Midland and it won't be back until tomorrow."

In the third seat, Vicky had tugged Brad's shirt out of his trousers and was rubbing some of the topical anesthetic cream Jared had given her over the staples in Brad's side. She winced as she felt the metal heads of the staples, though Brad didn't display any outward reaction. The anesthetic was a blessing, and the fragrance was soothing to him as well.

Brad, his pain eased by the anesthetic cream, was beginning to enjoy the feel of Vicky's hands on his bare skin, and he didn't notice that they were not headed for downtown Dallas until Grainger turned off onto the interstate.

"Where did you say you were taking us?" he asked.

Grainger turned his head and gave them all a sly smile.

"Like I said before, I'm taking you to Mrs. Ving. The location is a surprise. Just relax, please. It's about a thirty-minute ride and when we get there, I can assure you that you'll agree that it was worth the wait."

Roughly thirty minutes later, Grainger turned onto a long driveway lined with majestic cottonwood trees that had to have been planted seventy years before. The driveway wound its way over a rolling forty-acre pasture and up to a pretty, white, two-story Victorian house with a wraparound porch. The trim was painted a glossy dark green, and there were a couple of wooden swings painted the same green hanging suspended by chains from the ceiling visible on the porch. Grainger followed the driveway around to the rear of the house and parked next to a shiny new Mercedes in front of what appeared to be at least a six-car garage painted to match the house.

"What is this place?" Jessica asked, her eyes huge in her pretty face as she stared around the back. In addition to the huge garage, there was an enormous barn, a stable, a carriage house, a long, low bunkhouse, and a collection of outbuildings of various sizes, all painted the same as the main house.

A screen door at the back of the main house slammed shut, and the team turned as one to see a smiling Willona Ving hurrying toward the Excursion. Ving, of course, was the first one out of the SUV.

"Baby!" he called out, moving toward her with a smile on his face and his arms spread wide.

"Don't you 'baby' me, Mason Ving," she scolded. "You been back in Texas *how* long … and you didn't bother to call me to tell me you were back and okay?" Her tone of voice belied the smile on her face as she wrapped her slender arms around her husband and gave him a huge smack on the lips.

"Baby, I—"

"Shut up and kiss me, Ving, before I really do get mad and embarrass you in front of your team," she said without taking her lips from his. Everyone on the team was grinning hugely.

* * *

"He's *giving* this to me?" Brad asked incredulously.

"*Us*, Brad, he's giving it to *us*," Willona said. "And he didn't exactly *give* it to us. He took your apartment, your warehouse, and *our* house in trade."

Ving stared at his wife in shock.

"*Our* house?"

"Relax Ving, I had the lawyers draw up a separate deed for the carriage house and a right of first refusal on the forty acres behind it should Jacobs & Ving ever decide to dissolve. It will take some remodeling, but it's already really nice inside. Wait till you see the boys' rooms."

"Willona, this place has to be worth twice as much as our properties," Brad said, stunned.

"Ha! A lot you know, Brad Jacobs. This place was appraised at ten times the total of our properties, but you don't have to worry, those lawyers are slicker than goose snot."

"What do you mean?"

"I mean this place didn't cost Duckworth a damned dime. He inherited it lock, stock and barrel from his uncle. Worse yet, those lawyers are chomping at the bit to tear down that warehouse of yours and they're already buying up the others around it. Seems they have a development plan for some condos or something that they can barely wait to get started on. Those people don't waste any time."

"Holy shit, Willona! You done good!" Brad said, dumbfounded.

"That ain't all, Brad Jacobs," Willona said. "That new Excursion comes with the place. What do you think about that?"

"I don't know what to say, Willona, I'm ... speechless."

"Say thank you, Brad," Vicky murmured, standing up on her tiptoes to kiss him.

"Thank you, Willona," he said against the soft press of Vicky's lips.

"You are welcome, Brad Jacobs. Welcome home."

"Baby," Ving asked plaintively, "did you bring any of my bacon?"

*** THE END ***

EXCLUSIVE SNEAK PEEK: TRACK DOWN EL SALVADOR – BOOK 6

Thirty men dressed in black with an odd gold emblem embroidered on their sleeves descended on the tiny hamlet outside Soyapango with blood in their eyes. They were loaded for bear, armed to the teeth with suppressed automatic weapons, sidearms, fragmentation grenades, and explosives. Everything, in short, needed to start, and finish, a small war. Automatic weapons fire from unsuppressed weapons could be heard throughout the sleepy little village, and terrified residents raced out into the streets to see what was going on only to be cut down where they stood, open-mouthed and shocked . . .

A Brad Jacobs Thriller Series by Scott Conrad:

TRACK DOWN AFRICA – BOOK 1

TRACK DOWN ALASKA – BOOK 2

TRACK DOWN AMAZON – BOOK 3

TRACK DOWN IRAQ – BOOK 4

TRACK DOWN BORNEO – BOOK 5

TRACK DOWN EL SALVADOR – BOOK 6

TRACK DOWN WYOMING – BOOK 7

Visit the author at: ScottConradBooks.com

Printed in Great Britain
by Amazon